the *Not Yet* series

Until Now

a novel by

LAURA WARD

Copyright © 2016 by Laura Ward
First Paperback Edition: April 2016

Library of Congress Cataloging-in-Publication Data

Ward, Laura
Until Now (a Not Yet series novel) — 1st edition
ISBN-13: 978-1532888205 | ISBN-10: 1532888201

dedication

This book is dedicated to those
who have lost a loved one to suicide.
Siblings, friends, parents, and children…
your pain is never-ending. But you move forward, live your life,
and keep them with you always.
Bravery can come in the smallest of steps.

chapter
One

Dean

"SON, I GOT a call about an hour ago. A couple of NFL scouts are coming to the game this Saturday. The guy I talked to said you're looking like a first- or second-round draft pick." Coach K sat back in his chair with his thick, burly arms crossed over his chest. "*If* you keep up your current numbers."

Coach K had been the head coach of Indiana University's football team for the past fifteen years. The man was a legend. Back in the day he was a star player for his college team and then went right into coaching, helping to bring several teams to the national championships. He was also the scariest mother-fucker I knew. He allowed no bullshit from his players and doled out punishment workouts like a dentist gave out toothbrushes. Oh, and the man never smiled. Ever.

The corners of my lips turned up, but I kept my expression serious. "Yes, sir. I'll be ready."

Coach squinted at me and then took off his baseball cap, dragging his fingers through his bushy white hair. "Do you know what this means, Dean?"

I cleared my throat. "Team's having a great year, and I've got a shot at the pros." It was October, and the fate of the college football season was pretty much decided. Indiana University was known for its Big Ten basketball team, but football was holding its own this year.

Coach nodded. "You do. A serious shot." He leaned forward in his chair and placed his hands on his desk. "Don't fuck up, Goldsmith. You have three months to stay aggressive. Stay focused. This team is your family. That's all you need. Football comes first—before the parties, the girls, the booze. This is your one chance. Give it all ya got."

My hands started to shake, and I balled them into fists at my side. "Yes, sir. I understand."

Coach waved me out of his office with a grunt. If that's how the man acted when he had good news for me, I couldn't imagine how he would act with bad news. I never expected emotion from Coach K, but a part of me hoped I had made the crotchety old dude proud. He believed in me enough to make me his starting quarterback for the past two years, and that spoke volumes.

I walked out the door of IU's athletic complex and pulled out my phone to shoot my teammate Jon a text.

Me: *On my way*

My phone buzzed.

Jon: *New place today. Maria's Diner on Third. Heard food's ridiculous.*

My phone buzzed again, and I grinned when I saw the caller's name. Landon Washington.

"What's up, dickweed?" Landon and I had been friends for my entire life. Our humor, however, had never matured past the fifth grade.

Landon laughed at my greeting. "Not much, a-hole. I wanted to check in. Great game on Saturday. You're looking real solid."

I grunted in response. Coach K and I had discussed the possibility that I could go pro since scouts started showing up at my games last year. Still, saying it out loud felt like I could jinx it. Landon knew better than most people that I'd wanted to be a professional football player since my dad first put a ball in my hands. He also knew I'd stop at nothing to make it happen.

My best friend attended the University of Southern California. He was a second-string running back for the team, a huge feat for a walk-on player at a school like USC. But Landon was not headed for the pros. He had different goals for his future, and he played for the love of the game alone. Of course, if he'd attended IU with me, his story might have been different. We could have played like we had on our state-championship high school team with me as the quarterback and him as my best running back. But Landon made—in my humble opinion—the biggest mistake known to man.

He fell in love.

With a girl.

When he was eighteen.

"Sorry about your loss. That was a tough game." Landon's season was not going anywhere near as well as mine. He groaned, making a sound that I took as disgust, so I moved the hell on to his favorite topic. "How's Emma? You still pussy whipped?"

Landon snorted. "Shut the fuck up. I'm just smart enough to know that Emma's the whole damn package."

I crossed Tenth Street and waved to a group of sorority chicks as they headed back onto campus. "As long as she's taking care of your whole package, dude." Landon cussed into the phone, and I laughed. He was such a softie when it came to that chick. Hell, he'd followed her across the country.

"How about you? Met anyone yet? Some sweet, slightly disturbed chick brave enough to try and tie the infamous Dean Goldsmith down." I pulled the phone away from my ear at the sound of his guffaws.

"You crazy, Landon?" I said as I put the phone back to my ear, lifting my chin in greeting to two freshmen football players as they passed by. "You might be dumb enough to get shackled to one woman, but I'm smarter than that. Plenty of girls keep me warm at night, but they know better than to expect anything more." A wide grin spread across my face as I remembered Tuesday with Marissa, Thursday night with Leslie, and last night with Tracy...

Life was fucking good.

"Just wait, Dean. One of these days you're gonna change your tune. And when that day comes, I'm gonna sit back, crack a cold one, and enjoy the show." Landon's voice muffled as he spoke to someone else. "Gotta go, man. Emma's home."

Pussy. Whipped.

When that boy fell, he fell hard and fast. And for good.

Sucker.

Tied down to one girl? That would never be me. Tied up to the bedposts by a girl? Good possibility. I shook my head to erase that enticing thought. Right now I needed grub and some time with my boy, Jon. I opened the door to Maria's Diner and approached my teammate. Jon and I had also grown up together, playing ball in high school along with Landon. "What's up?" I smacked Jon on the shoulder as I slid into the booth. "You order yet?"

"Hey, man." Jon raised his chin and put his phone down. "A few things to start. I'm fucking starving."

"Coach K's practices are killer, but this is it. Senior year and I'm going all in." If it was going to happen, it had to be this year. This season. This was my time.

"Hell yes, thank you." Jon moved his phone out of the way, and a basket of cheese fries, mozzarella sticks, wings, and a large pepperoni pizza were placed on the table along with a pitcher of soda.

My stomach grumbled loudly. "This is starters? You're a pig, man."

Jon grinned as he shoved a handful of fries into his mouth and chewed.

"Thank you," I said as I looked up at the waitress.

Holy shit.

Dark green eyes narrowed at me, and I swallowed hard. I couldn't tear my eyes from hers. She cleared her throat, and I snapped out of it. I turned my head and was caught off guard by her hair. A thick braid hung down the front of her shoulder in the deepest shade of red I had ever seen.

"Can I get you anything else?" Her voice was clipped, and I immediately searched through the catalog of women I'd had sex with in my brain. Had we hooked up? Made out? Had I propositioned her? Bought her a drink?

My gaze traveled down her body. Creamy white skin covered in tiny brown freckles. She was thin but had tits. Killer legs and a great ass too from what I could see. No fucking way. I would absolutely remember bagging her. I'd remember that skin, those eyes, and that hot-as-hell hair. No way would I forget her. Time to make my move.

"Sorry, baby." I looked back into her eyes and smirked. "I got sidetracked for a minute. I almost lost my appetite for food… unless you're on the menu. I'd definitely like to taste you." Leaning back against the booth, I rested my arm along the top and tapped my fingertips on the red vinyl.

"Excuse me?" She took a step back and crossed her arms over her chest.

Jon barked out a laugh, and I gave him the finger. She sounded pissed. *Giddy-up.* I loved when they played hard to get.

"What's your name, sweet girl?" My previous douche bag come-on line was meant to make her laugh. Probably not my smartest idea being that I didn't know anything about this chick and she sure as shit didn't know me. If she did, she'd most likely be sitting in my lap by now. I poured some soda into the empty cup in front of me and took a long drink. When she still hadn't spoken, I glanced back up. She was gone.

"Losing your touch, bro." Jon wiped his fingers on a napkin and grabbed a wing. "Eat up, or it'll be gone."

Grabbing a slice of pizza, I folded it in half, took a large bite, and grumbled, "What the fuck? Uptight princess."

"Maybe she's not into you. Ever think of that?" Jon grabbed another wing and smirked. "Have you ever been turned down?"

My eyebrows furrowed, and I knocked my fist against the table. "Nope."

"So glad I was here to witness it then. Indiana's star quarterback can't even get the first name of his waitress. Love this shit. I gotta text Landon." The douche picked up his phone and typed, his big, sloppy fingers moving across the screen.

I drummed my fingers on the table, letting him have his fun. I had no insecurity when it came to my ability to get girls. If this chick wasn't interested, there was something wrong with her, not me.

Nevertheless I looked up, searching for her. She stood behind the bar, pouring a cup of coffee. Her face was pinched, and her shoulders slumped. I rubbed the back of my neck. Was she a college student at IU? She approached a nearby table and delivered the cup of coffee. The white-haired man sat alone but smiled at the sight of her. Her face relaxed as she bent down and spoke with the gentleman. I wondered if he was a regular. He reached out and patted her arm, and she nodded. Her smile dimmed as she stood up and looked around the crowded restaurant. One of my younger sisters, Dianna, was a waitress at a restaurant in the town where she was attending college. She had told me the work could be brutal, and this chick looked bone-tired.

I turned my attention back to our table, but not before she caught me staring at her. *Be cool, asswipe.* Jesus, was I in elementary school? I grabbed the last slice of pizza and watched Jon inhale the rest of the food on the table.

Jon wiped his face and pushed his empty plates to the side. "How's Daisy?"

Immediate pressure filled my head, and I cracked my neck to release it. "Why the fuck are you asking me about my sister?"

Jon glared at me. "Get a grip. She's a seventeen-year-old kid. I'm not hitting on her." He leaned back in the booth. "Last time we were home she told me about some girls giving her a hard time in school."

"What? Why did she tell *you* this?" I tightened my jaw. My sisters and brothers—all five of the fuckers—meant the world to me. I didn't say stupid shit like that to them, but they knew it. We had each other's back.

Jon held up his hands, palms facing me. "Settle. She tried to. You were sucking face with some chick. I handled it—"

"Hey there, hottie," a voice from beside us interrupted Jon.

I smiled before I even turned my head. "Hey yourself, Tues—Marissa." Christ that was close. When I had a semiregular rotation of girls that I saw, I referred to them by the day of the week we hooked up. Classy? Not a bit. Practical? As fuck.

My Tuesday-night hookup leaned over the table, her low-cut top showing off a shit-ton of cleavage.

"Wanna stop by my place tonight?" She spoke loudly, not trying to hide her words. I liked Marissa—she asked for exactly what she wanted.

"Maybe, darlin'. I haven't decided on my plans just yet." I reached up and tugged on a strand of her hair, and she laughed, giving me her best come-hither look.

"Excuse me."

I looked over Marissa's shoulder at our waitress. She placed our check on the table, and Jon held up one finger.

"Hold on one second. I'll give you my card." Jon reached back, digging in his jeans for his wallet.

Marissa stood up. Standing next to our waitress, she didn't look quite as cute as I remembered. *Her boobs fuckin' rock, but other than that...*

"Hey, I know you." Marissa chomped on her gum. "We have a psychology class together. You're always sitting in the front, taking notes." Marissa twirled the strand of hair I had tugged around her finger.

Our waitress stared at her for a second more than was comfortable. This chick did not care if she was rude. It was kind of refreshing.

"Right. Isn't that the point of class? To take notes?" the waitress asked Marissa.

Marissa wrinkled her nose. "Why? Can't you just listen?"

The waitress shrugged. "I don't have hyperthymesia. I guess you do."

Marissa's entire face scrunched up. No. She was definitely no longer cute. "Hyper what?"

The waitress widened her big green eyes. "I'm shocked. Hyperthymesia is the ability to remember every detail of your life. Professor White discussed it on Friday in class. You're welcome to borrow my notes if you'd like."

Marissa snorted and rolled her eyes at the waitress. "See you soon, Dean." She forced a smile in my direction before she stomped out the door.

Jon chuckled and handed our waitress his credit card. "You handled her. I've never seen Marissa back down to any girl before."

"I'm not any girl who cares about stuff like that I guess," she said and then looked down at the card. "I'll run this for you right now."

I couldn't wipe the grin off my face if I tried. The uptight princess was smart. And funny in a nerdy way. Marissa was one of IU's most popular cheerleaders. Like Jon said, I'd never met a girl who wasn't intimidated by her.

When she came back with the receipt, I placed my hand on her elbow. "I'm gonna need your name and number, darlin'."

I watched her hand Jon the receipt, wait for him to sign it, and purposefully ignore me. She took the signed receipt back from him, and I grinned up at her. "Well? You want to text it to me?" I asked, holding up my phone.

She tapped her finger on her chin. "Why don't I stick with my note-taking and table clearing, and you stick with football and... Marissa. That makes a lot more sense, don't you think?" She winked and walked off, her hips swaying in an infuriatingly sexy way.

Well, damn. There's a first time for everything, and I think I just got schooled.

Learning the name of an uptight, snarky waitress just became my favorite game to play.

Other than football, of course.

chapter
Two

Grace

WHAT THE HELL? Dean Goldsmith was flirting with me—
totally checking me out. How had I even gotten his attention?
Sure, I had guys ask me out all the time. Some were persistent,
but a cool brush-off and my stiff posture usually made them give
up rather fast.

At no time had anyone like Dean hit on me. The guy was a
man-whore. Gorgeous, but a player to the core. Stories about
Dean's sexual prowess were legendary on campus. Tall, blond,
and blue-eyed, you couldn't just ignore him and pretend he
wasn't in the room. He commanded attention wherever he went
by both his size and his laid-back attitude. He was flirtatious, a
party animal, and from what I could tell easygoing. Ha! He and I
weren't even living in the same universe.

"I'm out, Sylvie. I'll be back tomorrow at two."

Sylvie turned to me and smiled. At five feet two inches, her
petite frame and gray head of hair made some people misjudge
her as a softie. Talk to her for a more than a minute, and they'd

realize their mistake. Sylvie was direct and snippy to most people, but luckily she had a soft spot for me. My boss owned and managed Maria's Diner and was the toughest woman I knew. As a single woman who ran a busy diner seven days a week, she had no choice but to be tough. I respected her more than anyone else in my life. Her example was my mantra these days. Hard work pays off. *Stay strong, Grace.*

"Right," she asked. "You have classes until then?"

I nodded and slung my backpack over my shoulder.

"Don't run here and don't leave class early, Grace. You get here when you get here. School's most important." Sylvie turned back to her ancient computer where she slowly entered numbers into a spreadsheet. "Oh, and take that bag of food with you, girl." She motioned to a large brown paper bag.

I peeked inside and felt tears prick the corners of my eyes—bread, fruit, cheese, a jar of chicken noodle soup, and a box of muffins. This was enough food for the rest of the week. "You're the best." My voice cracked, and I swallowed the lump in my throat.

"I saw that boy watching you." Sylvie looked up from her computer. "The footballer."

"Really?" I cleared my throat. "I hadn't noticed."

Sylvie's eyebrows lifted high on her face. She kindly ignored my lie. "Why don't you go out with any of them? Boys like that baller ask you out all the time, and you've never said yes. Why? Doesn't need to be a big deal. You could catch a movie. I'd cover for you."

I twisted the end of my braid around my finger. I almost giggled when she called him a "baller." With her advanced age and lack of attention to anything modern, Sylvie spoke with an old-fashioned flair and a nod to her deep Southern roots.

"Sylvie, it's not happening. I've been burned before." I blew out a long breath. "I'm in Bloomington to get my degree. I have no need or desire to get close to a guy. Not now anyway." I stopped there before I said more than I should. The fact was, if I got close to a guy, I could get hurt by him. I would never allow that to happen again.

I picked up my bag of food. "Men are just a distraction from what really matters. I have to stay focused."

Sylvie studied me, not saying a word. Her lips were pursed, eyebrows pinched. I watched her expression change when she decided to let it go, and I felt lighter with relief. She turned back to the computer, intent on putting her digits in the spreadsheet she was working on. "Friday's special is meatloaf. I'll have a container of that for you to take for dinner." She didn't look at me as she typed, but she wasn't waiting for my response. Sylvie was one of the few people I never argued with. I couldn't. She only had my best interests at heart.

"Okay." I glanced at my watch, and my stomach sank. "Gotta go, or I'll be late." Sylvie waved me off as I grabbed the bag of food and headed out.

I adjusted my backpack and turned the corner. I would have to run if I was going to make it across campus by five o'clock.

"What's the rush, princess?" None other than Dean stepped in front of me, blocking my path.

I sighed. I didn't have time for this shit. "Excuse me." I sidestepped to the right, and Dean moved with me.

"What's your name?" He grinned down at me from his tall, lean but muscular frame.

"I'm sorry, I don't have time to talk. I need to go." I moved to the left and began walking. Dean turned around and began walking with me.

"Let me buy you a drink to loosen those lips. Maybe then I can learn your name? It must be god-awful if you're so hesitant to tell me. What is it? Matilda? Francine? My best friend has an aunt named Agnes." He grimaced and then chuckled. "That it?"

I could tell he was trying to be funny, but I looked away, grinding my teeth. "No time for the drink." I bit the words out and took a step backward.

Dean's chiseled face contorted in confusion. "You won't even meet me at a bar? We can hook up there later if you're busy now."

I rolled my head back and looked up at the sky. *Patience, Grace.* "No. I won't meet you at a bar. Not now, not later, not ever. I don't hang out at bars." *And I don't hang out with guys like you,* I thought. "I have to go." Dean stopped in his tracks, his eyes wide with shock. I used the opportunity to pass him by and sprint down the street, turning toward campus and slowing my jog when I realized he had given up his pursuit.

TWENTY-FOUR HOURS LATER I'd forgotten all about Dean Goldsmith. I concentrated on the reason I was here at IU—school.

My last class of the day was Art History. The elective course was a nice break from the business classes that were required for my major. I walked into Maria's and waved at Sylvie before heading to the back to change clothes.

Since meeting Sylvie during my freshman year of college when I had come looking for a job, she had arranged my work schedule around my classes. Without this job and her flexibility, I would've never been able to stay in school full time.

I clocked in and walked into the dining area, tying my apron strings behind my back. Sylvie motioned to a table, and I responded with a quick nod. Grabbing my pencil and pad of paper, I made my way over.

"Well, hello there." The hello was long and drawn out. I winced. Dean and his friend were back. His friend was wearing an IU football jacket, and I recognized him by his shaved head and close-cropped beard. Dean looked, as he always did, like a sexy surfer who had just rolled out of bed.

Probably some girl's bed.

His blond hair was disheveled in a way that made it seem like he didn't care when I was pretty darn sure he really did. His faded football T-shirt was snug in the arms and chest. God, his arms—I had a thing for arms. I liked them cut but not bulky, and I particularly liked tight, corded forearms. Dean had all that going on and then some.

I noticed cute guys before, but I'd never really been attracted to any. Dean's looks, personality aside, called to parts of me that had been dormant for years. He was a "take me to bed, no questions asked" kind of good-looking. Good thing I was the queen of questions and the furthest thing from a bed hopper. I squared my shoulders and shook off my lusty thoughts. *Never going to happen, Grace, so erase it from your mind.*

I looked over to see his friend watching me, an arrogant smirk on his face. He snickered in Dean's direction. "What can I get for you guys?" I asked.

"Cheesesteak sub and a coke for me." Dean's friend looked down, focusing on his phone, and I relaxed a bit.

Dean looked me up and down. "What's your favorite thing on the menu?"

I stared back. "Everything here is good."

"What's *your* favorite, Red?" His grin was slow to form and hot as hell.

Red. How original. "My favorite thing is the turkey club," I answered.

"That's what I'll have then. Oh, and a sweet tea and your name. What's your name, Red?"

I looked down. I'd forgotten my name tag again. A small smile slipped onto my face before I could stop it. "Red." I ducked my face to hide my blush, or more likely red cheeks, as I left to place their orders. I heard Dean's friend's loud laughter as I walked away.

As soon as their meals were ready, I delivered them with a smile. No matter how obnoxious the customer, I counted on the tips I made each day. "Can I get you anything else?"

Dean looked up with an impish grin. "Come with me to a friend's party Saturday night. I promise you'll have fun."

"No, thank you." I waved as Mr. Davidson walked in. He came in every afternoon for coffee and a Danish.

Dean's friend coughed the word "rejection" into his hand, and I held back my grin. Irritating Dean was kind of fun if I was being honest with myself. Turning down one of the top dogs at IU was amusing. I wasn't doing it to be mean. I truly had no interest or ability to go to a bar or a party with him.

Dean scowled at his buddy, then looked back up at me. "What's your deal, Red?" He cocked his head to the side and scratched his chin. "Everybody likes to party."

"Not me—unless by party you mean study. And I don't think that's what you mean at all, now is it?" I grinned cheekily when Dean's jaw dropped. "Enjoy your lunch, boys." I headed over to Mr. Davidson and caught Sylvie's worried glance. I waved her off with a smile. She didn't need to worry about me. I could handle the Dean Goldsmiths of the world.

chapter
Three

Dean

"DID YOUR MOM send pierogies?" Jon walked into the kitchen of our apartment with a big-ass grin, sniffing the air around him.

Damian laughed. "Sure did. Mom would never send me to Bloomington without your favorite dinner." He pushed the container laden with pierogi toward Jon. "Thanks for letting me crash here tonight, man."

"No problem." Jon pulled the foil from the casserole dish and shoved a whole pierogi in his mouth, groaning in satisfaction. "Fuck, yes. Still warm," he said around a mouthful of meat and potatoes. He swallowed before continuing. "Besides, you're Dean's little brother. You're family."

I leaned back in my chair. "Jon, no parties here tonight. He cannot be hungover when he meets with Coach K tomorrow. I'm serious. If he fucks this up, he'll end up at Purdue with the twins." Our brother and sister attended our rival school, and I had to make sure Damian got accepted here. Long-standing family competition and some serious ribbing were at stake. True, I was a proud party animal and a general asshole to my younger siblings, but I still looked out for them—especially when they were eighteen and visiting my campus.

Damian was hoping to get a football scholarship to IU like I had. My dad worked in a factory back home, so money was tight. Plus with six kids a year or two apart in age, my parents would have three in college at the same time for the foreseeable future. Scholarships were a necessity. I was pretty sure that Coach K wouldn't have asked him here if he wasn't planning on extending him an offer, but having my little bro show up hungover could change that plan real fast.

"I hear you." Jon shoved another pierogi in his mouth and then walked to the fridge to grab a beer. Giving Damian a nod, he twisted off the cap and handed it to him.

"Jerk-off? What did I just say?" I shouted and pulled the tray of pierogies over to my side of the table.

Jon grabbed the tray and held it over his head. "If you take these from me, I will kill you. They're that good."

Damian laughed and then took a long drink of beer. "Newsflash, bro. I've had beer before. Lots of it. You know, down at the river? Just like you used to do."

I couldn't argue with his point, so I grabbed a pierogi before my pig of a roommate polished them all off. "I know that. But tomorrow's important for you. Be cool."

Damian nodded, his face sobering. "Thanks for setting it up. I can't believe you're almost done playing at IU."

Reaching behind me, I opened the fridge door and grabbed myself a beer. "Me either."

"Can you call some chicks to come over tonight? A hookup would put me in a great mood before I meet Coach K." Damian waggled his eyebrows, and I threw my cap at his forehead. It landed dead center, and I barked out a laugh.

"No way in hell. Your Justin Bieber hair and tiny dick

would hurt my reputation." I grinned at the look on my brother's face as he smoothed his preppy hair.

"You're the small pecker in the family. My junk's so big girls tear up when they see me." He grabbed his crotch and tugged.

I rolled my eyes. "They're crying cause they can't feel shit."

Damian punched my throwing arm. Hard. *Fucker*. "You dating anyone or just hooking up with everyone?"

Jon licked his fingers as if in anticipation of what he was about to unload on my brother. "Your bro, the ladies' man that he is, has an honest-to-God crush on a girl that can't stand the sight of him. She won't even tell him her name."

"What? Fill me in." Damian rubbed his hands together in anticipation.

"I don't have a crush, nutsack. I just want to know her eff-ing name, and she won't tell me. It's driving me crazy." I dragged my fingers through my messy hair and finished my beer in one gulp.

"Where'd you meet her?" Damian asked.

Jon folded his hands behind his head and smirked. "She's a waitress at a diner. She's a knockout redhead. And she isn't buying what our man is selling."

Damian laughed too loud and too long for my liking. I smacked the back of his head. The last thing I needed was my dad, coach, or my annoying brothers and sisters figuring out that anything was distracting me from playing ball this fall.

But they wouldn't. Because there were no distractions. There was only football.

FIVE HOURS LATER Damian was passed out in my room, and Jon and I were well past shit-faced. I threw the controller of our

Xbox down on the table and fell back against the couch. "Fuck, I'm drunk."

Jon laughed through half-mast eyes that didn't seem to be focusing. "Me too. Isn't it great?"

"Not in the morning it won't be. Especially when we have sprints at seven o'clock."

Jon threw me a can of beer, and I popped it open. "We're this far gone, let's have one more." He opened his can and held it up in salute.

I saluted him back with a belch. My phone buzzed, and I read the screen with one eye closed. I found closing the one eye steadied my eyesight when I was inebriated. "Christ. It's Steph again."

Jon sat up in his recliner. "Steph's been calling?"

I tossed the phone to the side. "Only since she heard I might go pro." Stephanie Romley had been my on-again, off-again high school girlfriend. We were mostly off, leaving me plenty of time to hook up with interested females, but Stephanie and I tended to go to dances and other important events together. We were in the Homecoming Court from freshman to senior year and Prom King and Queen. We were never anything serious, but she was hot, easy, and wild as fuck. Now that she got wind of my money and fame potential, she was up my ass sideways.

"Gold digger. Seriously though, you're gonna have to be on the lookout for users. Girls are going to do anything they can to get with you in hopes of becoming an NFL trophy wife."

I took a long gulp of my beer. "I'm not the smartest, but even I can see through that plan. Never gonna happen."

Jon grabbed a handful of corn chips and shoved them in his mouth. How the hell was that guy still hungry? Sure, we burned a ton of calories each day in football, but Jon was always eating. Non-fucking-stop. I think he'd polished off twenty pierogies at dinner, and that was nasty no matter how good my mama made them.

"You can still lose it all. Look at Landon," he mumbled around half-chewed chips.

I sat up, placing my beer on the coffee table, and rubbed my eyes with the palms of my hands. "You don't think that runs through my head all the time? Jesus, man. He fucked up so big. He could be sitting here with us right now." I slammed back the last of my beer. "But he chose a girl over football at IU with you and me. I would never be that dumb. I'd never lose my career over a chick."

"Bros before hoes." Jon laughed.

And football above all.

I RAN MY fingers through my wet hair. Mission accomplished. I didn't puke after my workout this morning, and that was achieved by pure luck. I felt like dog shit when I woke up, but luckily Damian did not. Coach said he did fine during his interview, which for Coach was a rave review.

Yes, Coach had told me football first, but I had a few vices. Number one was beer with the boys. As long as he never found out, what was the harm? I survived the workout and had time to grab a shower before my nine o'clock American Studies class.

American Studies.

The class was total bullshit, but if I could get an A analyzing *How I Met Your Mother* and *Survivor*, then I was all in.

I walked up the steps to Ballantine Hall and felt a tap on my back. I looked over my shoulder. *Leslie.* Tall, blond, curvy, and *flexible.* Leslie made last Thursday night beyond good for me.

"Hey, handsome," she purred into my ear, and my lonely dick stirred to life.

Vice number two were girls just like Leslie. Ones that eagerly told me their name and wanted nothing more than to call mine out at night—because of what we did together in bed. That's all.

I turned to face her, and she pressed up against me, wrapping her arms around my waist. I rested my hands on her hips. "Hey, yourself." That was enough small talk for the lovely Leslie as she moved her lips against mine, slipping her tongue in before I had a chance to take control of the kiss. I wasn't a fan of girls who shoved their tongue in my mouth, but at least Leslie knew what she was doing.

I pulled away, and she stuck out her bottom lip in a pout. "Don't be mad, sugar," I whispered into her ear. "I've got a class now, but I could always meet up with you later. Text me." I bit the lobe of her ear, and she moaned. Loudly.

I heard a snort—one that sounded oddly indignant—and looked to my side to see who it came from. A redhead was walking up the stairs with her eyebrows raised high on her face. *Is that my waitress? Red? And what the fuck was that look for?* I opened my mouth to ask her just that, but lovely Leslie took that moment to give her parting farewell by re-inserting her tongue. I kissed her for another minute, and when I looked behind me, Red was gone.

"Bye, sugar." I kissed Leslie's cheek and ran into my class as the professor started her presentation.

For the life of me I couldn't concentrate. The subject was a damn television sitcom, and I still couldn't focus. Red's condescending look when she saw me with Leslie had my blood boiling. *Who the fuck does she think she is?* The princess thought she was too good for me. Her daddy probably warned her off football players. Or was she just playing hard to get?

I couldn't let it go, and that irritated me further. This was stupid. I could get any girl I wanted on campus. Why did Red's rejection piss me off?

As soon as the professor ended class, I grabbed my backpack and charged out the door. I headed straight for the diner. I didn't know her schedule, but I knew I wouldn't calm down until she told me why she disliked me without even knowing me.

Maria's was empty. A few customers sat with cups of coffee, but I supposed ten fifteen in the morning on a Wednesday wasn't prime time for meals.

"Excuse me?" I asked a petite woman with gray hair and tiny wire glasses, who sat on a stool at the hostess stand. "Can you tell me what time the waitress with red hair will be working?"

The woman's mouth flattened into a line. She narrowed her eyes and studied me. "What's her name?"

Shit. Wasn't that the question of the week? "I'm not sure." I held my breath hoping I sounded relaxed when inside I was geared up like a champ.

"If you don't know her name, I'm not telling you anything about her."

The woman looked back at her newspaper, and I groaned. "Seriously?"

She snapped her head up and pointed a pencil at my face. "I'll tell you what's serious, boy—that girl. She's as serious as they come. She's also the best person I know, so I'm warning you right now to back off. If she doesn't want anything to do with you, then stay the heck away. You are not what that girl needs right now."

A knot formed in my stomach at her words. *I wasn't what she needed right now? What did that mean? Who didn't need to relax and have a little fun?* I stared at the woman for a beat and then headed back out the door.

I left with more questions than answers. I was less pissed but decidedly more determined. I was going to figure out Red and find out exactly what it was that she did need.

chapter
Four

Grace

CRAP. I WAS late. I couldn't afford to be late. I ran faster, holding on to my bag of food from Sylvie. I was gasping for air as I ran into the doors of IU's Early Education Center.

"Hi, Grace!" One of my favorite faces, a smiling round one with bright pink glasses bounded up to me.

"Hey, Amy! How was Finn today?" Amy hooked a thumb over her shoulder, and I looked where she was pointing to see Finn sitting cross-legged on the multicolored rug stacking blocks.

"He was great. He always is." Amy grinned again. "How are you today?"

"Hanging in there. I have a bunch of homework tonight, so it'll be a late one." The longest part of my day was yet to come. Dinner, bath, stories, bedtime, cleanup, and then I could start my homework. Balancing Finn, a job, and classes left no time for anything else.

"Need any help? I can come over to play with Finn while

you work." Amy's normally happy face was concerned. She had been the teacher's aide in Finn's preschool and daycare class last year and this year. She was one of the most caring, gentle, and responsible people I had ever met.

"You know, I might take you up on that. I have a huge paper due in a few weeks. The only problem is, I don't have a car to pick you up." I could feel my face burn. I didn't pity my situation, but saying the words out loud made the realization that much more intense. I couldn't afford a car payment or insurance. Finn and I walked or took the bus.

"My parents and I live super close to campus. Mom can drop me off." Amy walked over to Finn's cubby and gathered his lunch bag and tote. Her father was a visiting professor at IU, so she told me her parents had rented a house in a neighborhood close to the university. "Remember," she handed the bags to me, "I got a daycare certificate for the work-study I did at Clemson." Amy pointed to a framed document on the wall, her smile beaming.

She should feel proud. Amy had been born with Down syndrome. It was rare for any person with intellectual disabilities to leave home and live on a college campus. Amy had done just that for two years. Once she completed her schooling, she was able to assist in early childhood classrooms.

"How did you learn about the work-study at Clemson University?" I asked, watching Finn play on the rug.

Amy shifted closer to me. "I never told you about that?"

I shook my head. Her smile turned proud as she pulled out a chair and sat at the craft table. "My senior year of high school I was an aide for the new, young teacher at my school. Miss Harris—I call her Emma now—was good to me. She talked to me and my parents about a program at Clemson for people just like me."

I had looked up her program at Clemson, curious why IU didn't have one like it. Clemson's curriculum was incredible.

During the two-year course, life skills and job training were taught to individuals with developmental disabilities.

"Are you still close with Emma?"

Amy nodded. "We get together whenever we are back home in Indy. She lives in California now with her boyfriend, Landon."

Finn looked up, and I waved. "Yay!" he called out after noticing me and jumped up, running over to where we were talking. Finn wrapped his small body around my legs. "I missed you when you were gone." He kissed my kneecaps, and I laughed away the happy tears that always formed when I saw Finn at the end of the day.

"I missed you too." I set my bags down and wrapped my arms around him.

"Squeezy hug!" he shouted, and we held on tightly to one another.

"Are you hungry for dinner?" I whispered into his ear as I knelt on the floor.

"My belly says, 'Feed me, now. I so hungry!'" Finn used a deep voice to give his best four-year-old monster impression.

I stood up and adjusted my backpack on my shoulders. Amy hung Finn's tote sideways across his body and slipped his lunch bag inside. I was then able to hold the food bag with one arm and Finn's hand with my other.

"Bye, Amy!" I called as we walked out the classroom door.

"Bye, Miss Amy!" Finn echoed, and Amy smiled and waved good-bye to both of us.

As we crossed the street, Finn pointed to the sky. "Can Batman fly?"

I grinned. Superheroes were the latest obsession in our home. I can honestly say I was glad to see Thomas the Train go. "Nope, just Superman."

Finn nodded and then let go of my hand, leaping in front of me. He extended his arms in front of him, legs spread apart and ready for flight. "When I grow up, I want to be a superhero." He took off running ahead of me, singing "Duntada, daaaa!"

Two girls sitting on a bench laughed as Finn ran by. A young child hanging out near the student dormitories on campus wasn't quite normal, but most of my peers were kind to Finn and understanding to me. We lived in a building designated as family housing, which really meant it was apartment style but at the cost of a typical dorm for single-parent families and married couples. I couldn't have made it through college any other way.

Finn opened the door to our building and held it for me. I stopped and crouched down to kiss his forehead. "Thanks, Super-Finn." He didn't need to wait until he grew up. He was already my hero. He didn't know it, but he saved me.

"You got it, Super-Mommy."

chapter
Five

Dean

MOMMY? DID THAT little guy call her super-mommy?

Holy hell.

My decision to show up today at the same time she had ended her shift the other day was impulsive. Following her so I could see what exactly her malfunction was, was decidedly stupid. What I never expected was for her to go into the campus daycare. Leaving with a kid, I figured she was babysitting. Then they walked to a campus apartment, and he called her "mommy." How the hell was she able to be a parent as a college student? Was she married? Was someone helping her? And why the fuck did I care?

This was why she turned me down. She had a damn kid. *Shit.* Her situation sucked, but it wasn't my problem. I had no time this year, of all years, to worry about Red and her kid. Nope. I had my priorities straight—football with a few vices thrown in for good measure. I texted Jon.

Me: *Meet at Patrick's for a beer?*
Jon: *Already there. Get your ass over here.*
Me: *On my way. Order me two.*

I needed a few beers pretty damn bad right now. The old lady was right. Red had serious shit to deal with. My most serious problem was making sure I didn't have a hangover for my morning workout.

My life was real fucking good. Damn near perfection. I had no room for complications or distractions.

Football first.

TWO BEERS BECAME four, and I had a nice buzz going while I mentally rehearsed plays for this Saturday's game. Jon and I sat at the bar, watching ESPN and eating peanuts. Patrick's was the toughest bar on campus to get into. The bouncers were legit, and everyone knew that if you posted at Patrick's with a fake ID, not only were you getting denied, you were also getting humiliated.

We went there to drink at least once a week because I enjoyed being able to hang out with an older crowd. I didn't have to deal with the fangirling or, hell, even fanboying that the younger students often did when they got to see their school's quarterback up close and personal.

"Can I buy you a beer?"

I looked to my left at the question. A guy in his early thirties I'd guess, with slicked hair and a three-piece suit, stood at the bar. He took a long sip of his martini and eyed me up and down.

"Nah, I'm good. Thanks." I nodded and turned back to the television. He was probably an alumni member who wanted to talk football.

A small white business card was placed in front of me. I

looked down and saw "Andrew Johnson, Sports Agent" in black block lettering. I snapped my head up. I didn't recognize his name, but I knew what his title meant. He had my attention.

"I can't actually be here right now, Dean, but I wanted to be the first to meet you." He extended his hand, and I shook it. "Andrew," he introduced himself, and I motioned to the seat next to me.

He pulled out a stool and sat down. "You'll have to pretend we never had this conversation. I'm supposed to go through your school at agent player week. But Dean." Andrew took another drink of his martini. "I'm hearing a lot of buzz about you."

"What buzz is that?" I took a long pull from my beer. My stomach felt like it was freefalling.

Andrew sat back in his chair. "You still graduating early?"

I nodded. "I've taken a few classes here and at home each summer. I've been hoping that I'd make it into the draft, and I know that means I can't take classes in the spring. The one thing my mom asked was that I get my diploma before I try to go pro. She worries." I grinned, and Andrew smirked in return.

"She shouldn't. You finish this season healthy and with a good record, and you're getting drafted. Early, I'd bet. Dallas and Chicago have started asking questions. They both need quarterbacks pretty damn bad."

Two professional football teams had asked about me? And Andrew was standing here talking to me? It was only October. This was real.

Andrew stood up. He threw a pile of cash on the bar, enough to cover his martini and several more beers for Jon and me. "I'll call you as soon as the eligibility list comes out. Meanwhile, I'll be at each game. Give me a shot to work with you, Dean. I'm already lining up endorsement deals. I can help you become a very, very rich man." He shook my hand as he spoke.

I could only nod.

Andrew left, and Jon ended his conversation with a brunette

standing next to him, who had more than an ample amount of rack. "Who was that?" Jon signaled the bartender for another round.

"An agent."

"No shit?" Jon passed me a beer, and I finished the one in my hand.

"Yup. Said Dallas and Chicago need quarterbacks. They've been asking about me." Jon's eyes got round, and then he grinned.

"Fuckin' awesome, Dean. Congrats, man." We clinked beers. "Now don't do anything to fuck this up. I mean it. Head in the game." Jon's words were about the same as Coach K's.

"Football's the only thing to think about," I agreed.

I stared down at my bottle. Thoughts of agents and deals and professional football ran through my head. And then I thought about Red and her kid. Here I was drinking a beer after hearing that every dream I had ever had could come true, and I was thinking about her. That little old lady was right. I wasn't what Red needed, and she sure as hell wasn't what I needed right now.

THE PERSISTENT VIBRATION of the phone next to my ear woke me the next morning.

"Hello?" My voice was groggy, and my throat was dry. I felt like crap again this morning.

"Dean?"

"Morning, Ma." I should have known. Only my mom would call at seven in the morning.

"Why aren't you up? Don't you have a morning workout? You sound terrible. Tell me you weren't drinking last night. It's a school night for goodness' sake." Mom rambled on, and I sat up, stretching and yawning.

"Settle down, Ma. I'm fine. Afternoon workouts today." I swung my legs out of bed and grabbed a bottle of water I'd left on my nightstand. "I met an agent last night who's interested in working with me."

"Really? That seems early. I know your dad will want to meet him. Don't sign anything until then." Mom spoke faster. I pictured her pacing our kitchen, coffee cup in hand, just home from her morning walk.

"Sure thing. I'll have him meet both of you. Just thought you'd like to know." I slipped on my athletic pants and walked into the kitchen to start the coffeemaker. "Is Daisy okay? Jon mentioned something…" I hoped I wasn't causing Daisy problems by asking Ma, but I had to know. If something needed to be handled, I would come home and deal with it.

Mom sighed. "She's okay. Some queen bees have been bullying her. She'll be fine. I'm on it. Delilah and Damian too."

My stomach dropped. I used to be quite the shithead at school. Maybe even a bully. The thought that someone could treat anyone in my family badly made my blood boil. "You let me know if you need me, yeah?"

"I will, son." I could hear the smile in her voice. She loved that her children all razzed one another but would never let anyone else hurt a hair on their head. "One last thing. Guess who came by last night?"

Shit. It could only be one person. "Uh, Steph?" I didn't like the girl, but right now I feared for her. My mom was intense.

"Yes," she huffed. "Can you imagine? She cheated on you all through high school, and then she has the audacity to show up at our home as soon as the rumors start about your career."

I bit my tongue to hold back my laughter. Only my mom would assume Steph cheated on her boy. There was no cheating when there was no commitment made.

"Don't you worry. I handled her. I told her you had no time

for a relationship, and even if you did, it wouldn't be with a money-grubber like her."

Whoa. Go mama bear. "How'd she take that news?"

"Oh, she was pissed, but she left. I think she realizes she'll never be a daughter-in-law of mine." Mom laughed into the phone.

I shuddered. Daughter-in-law? Maybe in twenty years I'd be ready for that. "Thanks for taking care of me, Ma. I love you."

"Be good, son. I love you too."

I poured a mug of coffee and then jumped in the shower. I always knew how lucky I was to have the family I was born into. A little reminder now and then was still pretty great.

EVEN A MILD hangover couldn't get Red off my mind. I was the one with the malfunction. I didn't want to bother her at work, but I remembered we had class at the same time. I got to Ballantine Hall early, hoping to catch Red and avoid Leslie.

I didn't see either. Now a full-fledged creeper, I waited on the steps after class, looking for Red. She rushed through the door, looked at her watch, and jogged down the steps. I went after her.

"Hey, Red," I called out to her, and she stopped, looking behind her.

Her eyes widened when she saw me. "Hi?" Her confusion made me smile.

"I'm Dean." I held out my hand, and she waited a beat before shaking it.

"I know who you are. Everyone knows who you are." Her scowl was seriously cute. The idea that my popularity made her upset, though, was weird.

"I just said hi, Red. How have I already pissed you off? It's…" I looked at my watch. "Only ten o'clock in the damn morning." I ran my hand through my hair. Her eyes followed the motion, and I fucking liked that she was looking at me without irritation for once.

She laughed as she blew out a breath. "I'm sorry. I'm not pissed, I'm just not sure why you keep trying to talk to me. I saw you making out with that girl the other morning. In fact, I've seen you with lots of girls, so I know you aren't lonely. The fact that I've told you no must be the only reason you keep trying with me."

My eyebrows pinched together, and I took a step backward, holding my arms out to the side. "Hey, now. First off, I was only asking for your name." She raised one eyebrow, and I held up my hand to stop her. "Okay, and I asked you out for a drink and to a party. But that was before."

Her face fell, and she reared back.

I. Was. A. Fucking. Asshole.

"Before what?" Her voice was flat. She pressed her lips together, her eyes narrowing as she watched me.

Fuck. "I… didn't mean it like that." A group of football players slapped me on the back, shouting out greetings as they headed toward the building. American Studies was popular with the jocks. I turned back to her, but she was walking away at a fast clip.

I had to apologize. I already knew she wasn't like the other girls at school, and I didn't want her to leave with her feelings hurt.

"Wait! Wait up." I ran to her, and she turned around—her face was red. It was such a contrast to her pale skin. Like her anger was a physical being, the color altered her face so drastically. "I want to explain, but I need to know your name. I'd like to apologize the right way."

Her red flush traveled down to her neck, and when I looked

into her eyes, they were full of tears. *Motherfucker*. I was seriously the lowest common denominator.

"Grace. My name is Grace. I need to go, Dean. I don't want to be here right now." Her hand shook as she pulled her hair away from her face.

I took a step closer, wiping my sweaty hands on my jeans. "I followed you yesterday." Her jaw dropped open, but I continued. "I was only trying to get you to talk to me. Then I saw you go into the daycare center, and you came out with a little guy. He called you mommy."

She swallowed, not saying a word.

"Are you a full-time college student?"

She nodded.

"And you work at Maria's Diner?"

This time, I got a slight jerk of the head.

I looked at her hand, where there were no rings, but I still asked. "Are you married?"

She closed her eyes and shook her head.

"So, you're a, uh… a single mom?" Her lips flattened, and she straightened, narrowing her eyes. For a second I thought she might just walk off and leave me standing here.

"Why do you want to know?" Her voice had an edge to it. She was still pissed off.

I blew out a breath and rubbed the back of my head. "You're a tough cookie, Red. I'm only asking if you need anything. Doing it all by yourself must be hard. Damn, I wish my family lived closer. I've got a bunch of sisters that babysit and shit all the time." *What was wrong with me?* I kept babbling… word vomiting all over this girl. But I couldn't stop. "I just feel… sort of… bad… for you."

Her face deepened to a shade of crimson that scared the shit out of me. She stalked forward, and I instinctively moved back.

"I." She shoved a finger in my chest. "Don't." She jabbed again. "Need." Poke. "Anything." Poke, poke. "From." Jab.

"You." She raised her finger to my face, and I couldn't tell if she was going to hit me or cry. I did know I had hurt her pretty badly.

She turned and walked away.

"Grace, wait! I wasn't trying to be a dick!" I shouted and started after her, but she took off running.

I needed to let her go. She wasn't ready to hear any more stupid shit coming from my trap. *Jesus.* Why did I offer to help her? Why did I care?

Grace was so completely different than any girl I knew. From high school through college I'd only ever hung around women who cared about their shade of nail polish or designer flip-flops. Grace was a mom. A hot mom, with her long red hair, curvy figure, and perfect heart-shaped face, but still. She was a college student who must have the weight of the world on her shoulders.

Me? I had football and beer, and girls who didn't care about attachments. They just wanted to be with me.

Walking back into my building, two hot chicks waved at me, but I ignored them. Blondes had always been my type. Now a fiery redhead was the one who'd gotten under my skin.

chapter
Six

Grace

"MEATLOAF? I LOVE meatloaf!" Finn ran into the kitchen wearing a cape and underwear. Comic book Avenger's underwear.

"Finn, I require pants when we eat meals." I poured his milk and my water, bringing both over to our small round University-furnished table.

Finn sat cross-legged on his chair. "I'm wearing pants, Mom."

I looked down again, lips curled to hide my grin. "No, you are not."

He speared a large broccoli floret with his fork. "Invisible pants."

I snort-laughed. I'd just been beaten by a four-year-old. I heard a knock on the door, and Finn leaped out of his chair, causing it to fall sideways on the floor. "Wait for me, Finn. Do not open that door." I picked up the chair and moved to the door. Which was open—and filled with Dean Goldsmith. What was he doing at my home? He was crossing some big lines these days.

"You're so tall and huge. Are you Captain America?" Finn's head was thrown back until it was resting on the back of his shoulders.

I wanted to answer for him. *No, son. He's Captain Dickhead.* But I refrained.

Dean laughed and crouched down to Finn. "Nope. My name's Dean. I like your cape. Are you Superman?"

Finn giggled and shook his head. "Mommy calls me Super-Finn, but I'm really just Finn."

"Hello, Just Finn. It's nice to meet you." Dean held out his hand, and Finn shook it, still laughing.

"Finn, you are not allowed to open the door unless I'm with you. There could be a stranger at the door." I paused. Dean was a stranger. Case in point. "This is a stranger, Finn. We don't know him at all. Please wait in your room until I know it's safe."

Two sets of eyes whipped to me. Finn's were full of guilt and confusion. Dean's were pissed and... was he hurt? He didn't get to look hurt. Not for one second.

"Okay, Mommy. I'm so... so... sorry." Finn's lower lip trembled, and I pulled him into a hug.

I placed my lips close to his ear and whispered. "It's okay. Just wait for me next time." He nodded and ran into his room. The sound of a toy bag being upended filled the space between Dean and me.

"That was a low blow, Grace. I'm not a complete stranger. I get that I'm a douche, but I'm not a dangerous one." Dean's tone was jovial, but his eyes were narrowed.

I placed my hands on my hips. How the hell did I know if he was dangerous or not? One lesson I'd learned early on was that men could hurt even those they loved. I wouldn't let any man hurt my son or me. Not ever again, intentional or not. "You might be. I don't know you. I know you followed me home, spied on me, and then offered to help me. Sounds super safe, right?" I moved my hands to my sides and walked over to him. "You need to leave. I have a child, which you know based on your superior stalking methods. I can't have you here."

Dean looked at the floor, a smile tugging at the corners of his mouth. "Never been called a stalker before." He reached into his back pocket and handed me an envelope.

My face burned with heat, and I forced myself to whisper and not scream like I wanted to. "What is this? I told you I didn't need anything from you. If this is money, I will call the police. And slap you. I will so slap the shit out of you."

Dean rolled his eyes. "I'm not that stupid. It's two tickets for tomorrow's game. I wanted to apologize and didn't know how. I said the wrong thing. I thought Finn might like to go to an IU football game," he said placing the envelope in my hand, curling my fingers around it to encourage me to accept it. My heart raced from the contact. I needed to calm the hell down.

He grinned, and my body relaxed. He was trying. I'd give him that. I placed the envelope back in his hand. "Thank you, but I don't have the money right now for concessions. Trust me, a four-year-old surrounded by popcorn, peanuts, and cotton candy will not be understanding when I say that Mommy left her wallet at home." I hoped to make light of my situation with a small smile, but his face fell at my words.

"I'm sorry to hear that, Grace. But these are in the family section. Free food and drinks. They'll even deliver it right to your seats. Come hungry." He winked, and a lump formed in my throat. It had been so long since anyone other than Sylvie had done something like this for Finn and me.

I bit my bottom lip and studied his face. "Why? Why are you being nice? What do you want from me?"

Dean reached out and brushed his thumb along my cheek causing me to jump in response. My heart raced as he stayed close to me, placing his lips close to my ear in the same way I had done with Finn. "I don't know exactly, but I like you. I don't want anything in return except your forgiveness. I'm sorry I hurt you."

I nodded, unable to form words. Dean squeezed my shoulder and moved back. He called out, "Bye, Just Finn! Hope to catch up with you soon, little dude."

"Bye!" Finn yelled back from his room, but Dean had already shut the door behind him.

I sat down at the kitchen table and took a long drink of water.

"Mommy?" Finn asked for my attention as he climbed back into his chair and took a bite of meatloaf. "Was he safe? Was that stranger a nice guy?"

I kissed Finn's forehead and nodded. "His name's Dean, and I think he wants to be my friend."

"That's nice. You don't have any friends." Finn dipped his next bite in ketchup and shoved it in his mouth.

The lump was back, and I swallowed around it. "I have you, buddy. I don't need anyone else."

I KNELT NEXT to the bathtub, dragging my hands through the bubbles. A bubble bath sounded heavenly. My feet ached from standing so long at the diner, and my back and shoulders were tight from hunching over books. There was no time for a bath. Not for me anyway.

"What's this?" Finn asked me, lying back in his tub.

I looked down and then stifled a giggle. "That's your penis, buddy."

Finn shot me a look that clearly told me my four-year-old thought he was smarter than his mother. "I know that. Why is it standing up straight like a soldier?"

Crap. A penis question. This was when not having a penis

became an issue. I didn't think he was ready... okay, I wasn't ready to use the word *erection*. I shuddered internally. He was four years old, for goodness' sake. Dumb it down. "Penises do that sometimes. It'll go away."

"M'kay."

I lathered his head with shampoo. How would his dad have responded to that question? God, I hoped I had the right answers.

I turned on the faucet, and Finn lay back against my arm as I ran the clean water over his shampooed head of hair. He closed his eyes, his complete trust in me and my safekeeping of him so humbling. Motherhood was its own kind of power, and while I never could have imagined the feeling that caring for this boy gave me, I promised myself I'd never do anything to jeopardize it.

"Mama? Our teacher told us that next week is Grandparents' day at school. Who will come to see me?"

I turned off the faucet and drained the tub. Finn stood, and I toweled him off. This wasn't the first time he had asked me about his grandparents, but it felt like it got harder to answer each time.

I held out Finn's underpants, and he stepped into them. "It's just you and me, buddy. Remember?"

Finn pulled his pajama shirt over his head, and when his face popped out of the top, his expression crushed me. At four years of age, he had learned to fake it. A halfhearted smile was plastered on a face that should know nothing but true joy. Unfortunately, life wasn't always kind.

Finn yanked up his pajama bottoms, and then I pulled him onto my lap. "You're my whole world, Finn. I'm going to school so I can give you everything you need. I'm going to take care of you. I promise." I kissed the top of his damp head. No amount of education and or any job could give him what he wanted though. A whole family.

Finn was all the family I needed. I was content to dedicate

my life to the one person that deserved it. Nothing had made me as happy as being his mom.

I just prayed I was enough for him.

FALL FOOTBALL GAMES were a tradition for many college students. As I walked to the stadium with Finn, I saw students bundled in red and white IU sweatshirts, some with blankets around their shoulders to ward off the chilly morning breezes. They huddled around the trunks of cars, passing beers around to all, despite the fact that it wasn't even lunchtime. The smell of charcoal grills filled the air as students and alumni cooked hotdogs, hamburgers, and bratwursts. Games were set up in the parking lot. Some played a game with beanbags while others tossed footballs back and forth. Conflicting beats and melodies from the various sound systems overpowered the chatter. My stomach filled with butterflies as I took it all in.

The scene was foreign to me. I was a college senior at a Big Ten university, and this was my first football game. I couldn't afford to go before, so it never crossed my mind. I had no idea what I had been missing.

Once inside the stadium, I eased my knees to the side so that a group of people could move past me to their seats. The family section was full of well-dressed, proud parents and siblings. A waiter knelt next to Finn's seat and passed soda to me and juice to Finn. "This is all free?" I whispered. My stomach dipped. I was so screwed if Dean had been wrong.

The waiter smiled in understanding. "Only in this section and the section for former IU athletes. Enjoy!" He passed two hotdogs, popcorn, and a soft pretzel to me. My stomach growled. I was starving, and junk food like this was a rarity for Finn and me.

"Thank you," I smiled in return. "We will."

Finn sat cross-legged in his seat, and I unwrapped his hotdog, placing it on his lap. Everywhere I looked there was excitement. Cheerleaders and dancers moved to the booming music, and students clapped and hollered. The stadium was a sea of red and white. Despite the cold, rows of guys were shirtless, the skin on their chests painted red, each with a single letter painted on it in white block lettering. Standing side by side their chests read: "GO IU! #1". Many students and visitors wore IU jerseys in red or white, hats in the same colors, and quite a few painted their faces. I couldn't keep the smile off mine. The energy was contagious.

"Mommy, this is so cool!" Finn held my hand tightly in his. He was smiling just like me and had a dollop of mustard from his hotdog on his chin.

I wiped his face with my napkin. "It really is!" Just then the IU football team was announced, and we stood with the rest of the stadium and clapped, whistling, and calling out as each player was called to the field by name.

"Where's Dean? I don't see him!" Finn stood on his chair, moving onto his tiptoes in an attempt to spot Dean.

I picked Finn up and sat him on my hip. "His name hasn't been called yet. Hold on..." I pointed to the entrance, and fireworks shot out of the ground as the announcer screamed Dean's name and number. I couldn't believe it. He really was the star player on this team. I knew he was cocky, but I didn't think there was an actual reason for him to feel that way.

"There he is! Hey, Dean! Hi! It's me, Just Finn!" Finn waved his hands in the air, and I giggled, loving every second of his excitement.

We moved to sit down as the players got organized on the field. "He can't hear you, buddy. We're too far away." I handed him his popcorn. "But he knows you're here."

Finn nodded and shoveled a handful of buttery kernels into

his mouth. He'd eat his way through the game and be as happy as could be. I loved seeing Finn so excited. I tried as hard as I could to make his world fun, but it was hard, and I was worn out. This gift from Dean was what we both needed.

We continued to devour our stadium food, stopping only to get to our feet and scream with excitement when Dean threw a pass or when IU's defense intercepted the ball. "Yes!" I jumped up along with the rest of the crowd to cheer as Dean threw the ball to his running back and he ran it in for a touchdown. In the previous play, Dean had gotten sacked, and I held my breath until I saw him get up. He hadn't looked hurt, thank God.

Finn asked me a ton of questions about the game, and I knew the answers to about ten percent of them. I'd need to study up on football. Finn didn't have a daddy to teach him sports. He didn't have anyone but me.

That thought used to scare me. Now it was what kept me going.

chapter
Seven

Dean

WHAT WAS WRONG with me? Sunday morning after our games, I usually woke up in bed with a girl—or two. Those were good times. This Sunday morning I was using Google Maps to search for a park near Grace and Finn's apartment. I'd shown up at their door with a bag of donuts, but they weren't home. A hot chick walking by told me they were at the park, but she didn't know which one. I also noticed the hot chick was wearing a wedding band. Who the fuck got married in college?

Laughter filled the air, and I walked faster. Sure enough, around the corner was a large playground surrounded by green grass and picnic benches. Grace was sitting on a picnic bench with her long red hair tied up in a bun. Finn was the dude who was laughing. He was sliding down the slide and then racing up the steps to do it again. The idea of hanging out with Finn felt natural to me. Maybe it was my big family? Being the oldest, I was used to being around younger kids. They were funny as shit, and hanging with my siblings always gave me a break from the stupid, petty crap that seemed to infest my life. I had a feeling being around Finn would be the same.

"Hey." I waved as I approached her table.

Grace jumped up, and her mouth dropped open when she saw me. Her eyes hardened, and a crease formed on her fore-head. "What the…?"

I slowed my pace. In actuality, this was the third time I had stalked this girl. *Balls.* I really was a creeper. I could only hope she wasn't carrying mace or a stun gun.

"Dean!" Finn raced toward me, hurling his body against my legs. "You're here! I'm so glad. Could you hear me at the game? I was calling for you! Mama and I cheered so loud when you threw that ball real good. You heard us, right?" His words came out so fast I had a hard time keeping up. He dragged in a breath, and I took the break to kneel on the ground.

"I couldn't hear you, Just Finn. But I knew you were there, and I was hoping you were cheering for me. Did you have fun?"

His face erupted into a blinding smile. "I had the best day ever. I ate a hotdog, popcorn, a pretzel, and cotton candy. I liked the marching band and those pretty cheer girls." His eyes got big when he mentioned the cheerleaders, and I threw my head back and laughed.

"You like the cheerleaders, Just Finn?" He nodded, and I looked up at Grace. She twisted her mouth, but I could tell she was smiling. "None of them are as pretty as your mom though." She pressed her lips together and looked away.

Finn reached over and grabbed his mom's pinky finger. "That's true. My mommy is the most beautiful in the world." At his words, Grace relaxed. She leaned down and kissed his lips, making a loud popping sound. They both giggled, and my chest tightened.

I stood up and handed the bag to Grace. "I brought donuts," I said, grinning when Finn whooped and then sat down at the picnic table like a perfect gentleman.

Grace's eyebrows rose high on her face. "Why?" She asked as she sat the bag down on the table.

"Why what?" I pulled out a stack of napkins and handed a few to Finn. He reached into the bag and placed three large donuts on his napkin. I liked this little dude more and more.

"Chocolate are my favorite! Yes!" Finn cheered.

"Why did you bring donuts? Why are you here? And how did you know where we were?" Grace took one donut off his pile and placed it back in the bag, shaking her head at Finn when he opened his mouth in protest.

I handed her a donut from the bag and then grabbed two chocolates for myself. I took a big bite, chewing, and swallowing before I answered her. "I was hungry. Felt like a donut. Thought you guys might too. And I asked your neighbor." I ate the rest of the donut in another two bites and moved on to the next.

Grace looked at the donut in front of her as if it could answer all these questions she had. "I never told anyone what park we were going to."

I grinned and held up my phone. "Google Maps rocks. Now eat that. It's called a cronut. It's what happens when a donut and a croissant breed." She laughed, and something inside me warmed. "I should have asked you what kind you like. Tell me what your favorite is so I know for next time."

Grace stilled, and she studied her hands.

"Well?" I reached into the bag and pulled out another cronut. "Cheers!" I knocked my pastry against Finn's, and he giggled. Grace looked between us and sighed, her shoulders sagging as she made her decision.

"I've always liked glazed." She took a small bite and let out a low moan. "But this might be my new favorite." She swallowed and then looked at me for a few seconds before speaking again. I could almost see her weighing her choices and trying to decide how to handle me. I wanted to laugh, but I was pretty sure I'd be ejected from the park if I did. "Thank you... Dean."

I winked. "This great company's thanks enough, Red. Now after this fuel, I want to check out the swings. Sound good, Just Finn?"

Finn squealed and high-fived me, his hands sticky with sugar and chocolate frosting. "Yes!"

Grace handed Finn his water bottle and a wipe. "Water?" She held up a bottle, and I nodded.

I took a long drink. Finn stood in front of me buzzing with energy from his sugar high. That was probably why Grace didn't let him eat that third donut. "I'll meet you on the swings, little dude. Give me five minutes." Finn nodded and raced back to the playground.

I turned to Grace. "I hope you aren't mad that I came here. I can't stop thinking about you." I couldn't. That was why I passed on a hookup last night and why I was at a playground park on a Sunday. This beautiful girl had some kind of hold on me.

"I don't want your pity, Dean. Finn and I are fine." She crumpled a napkin in a ball. Her body was stiff again, and her mouth flat.

Damn. That wasn't my intention. "No pity. None. But I do admire you. I think you're different from anyone else I've met here at college. I'd like to get to know you better…" Her face flushed pink, and she chewed on her lip. Aw hell, she was freaking out on me. "As a friend. I'd like to have friends like you and Finn." I took another drink of water. I felt desperate for her to agree. "If that's okay with you."

She studied my face before answering. "Okay. Friends." She didn't smile, but she also didn't seem angry or like she might hit me. That was a step in the right direction.

Yes! I wanted to pump my fist in the air, but I stayed calm. I could tell Grace rattled easily. "Okay." I reached over and squeezed her hand, still balled into a tight fist. Then I headed for the swings. I hadn't played on a playground in well over ten years. Hanging here with Finn, though, made for a pretty damn good Sunday morning.

"YOU'RE LATE." JON took a bite out of his hamburger, and I slid into the seat across from him. He chose the same booth, toward the back of the diner. I wasn't sure if Grace was working today, but the thought that I could bump into her again made my heart pound faster in my chest.

I grabbed a fry off his plate, ignoring his glare as I shoved it in my mouth. "Sorry. Workout went long today."

Jon wiped his mouth with a napkin. "Where'd you go yesterday? A couple of the guys and I did a bar crawl downtown. I texted you... never heard back."

Shit. I wasn't ready to tell Jon or anybody else about Grace and Finn. There was no way he'd understand, and if he gave me a hard time about her, I was pretty sure I'd punch him right in the face. "Out. Had stuff to do." I studied the menu and avoided my best friend. Growing up, I was close to four guys. Jon, Landon, Ricky, and I had been tight ever since we met in elementary school and ended up all playing ball together in high school. After we graduated, Landon went to school out West, and Ricky stayed home in Indianapolis, attending community college. Now we only saw each other during the summers and holidays.

Except for Jon and me. We were teammates and roommates. He knew everything about me. But I wasn't sure he needed to know this information.

"What stuff? Or were you *doing* Leslie? Mary? Chantal? The entire cheerleading squad?" Jon threw his balled up napkin at me and laughed.

"Hi... Dean."

Grace's voice was soft and hesitant. Hearing it made me

hard. Girls made me hard all the time but not from just speaking. I looked up at her, her bright red hair in a braid, face pale, save for the pink flush on her cheeks. I checked her out from head to toe. She wore the diner's old-school uniform. A blue and white dress with a white apron. On anyone else it would be dorky. On her? She looked fucking cute.

"Hi, Grace." I smiled, and her blush deepened. Her face changed color in time with her emotions. The times I'd watched her expressions and the color of her face change directly correlated with our conversations. Based on our interactions, I could tell the shade she would turn if she was shy, worried, or mad. I liked that it was kind of a window inside of her. I wanted to see more. What shade would she turn if I touched her? Kissed her?

Right now her blush seemed nervous, and I needed to figure out how to change that. I wanted Grace to feel comfortable around me. "How are you?" I asked her.

Jon looked back and forth between Grace and me, his eyes wide. Grace didn't smile back. Instead, she seemed stiff and kind of awkward. Again, it was fucking cute.

"I'm fine." She pulled out a pad of paper and a pen. "Know what you want?"

Damn that girl was cold. I thought after the park that we could at least talk to one another. "Are you working all day?"

Her eyebrows pulled together, and she stared at me in silence. "Working this afternoon, and then I have a class." She looked around the restaurant and chewed on her lip. "I have to get to another table. What can I get you to eat?"

I didn't look back down at my menu. "Surprise me." I handed it to her and rested my arm along the back of the booth.

Grace dipped her head and studied me again. I'd pay all the money in the world to get inside her mind for a few minutes.

"All right. I'll bring you the special." She turned to leave but stopped and took a deep breath before facing me. "I don't mean to be rude. Thank you again for the donuts. And for coming to the park. You made his day." She gave me a small lopsided grin that was so goofy it was adorable.

I was one hundred percent certain that a happy Grace was the most beautiful sight in the world. And I was learning that whenever Finn was happy, so was Grace.

"I had fun too." I reached up and squeezed her hand, but she yanked it away.

"Excuse me? Miss?" A customer waved to Grace.

She straightened, smoothing the skirt of her apron and nodded at the customer. "I'll put your order in."

I turned back to Jon, who sat, mouth open, hamburger in hand, staring at me. "What?" I snapped.

He closed his mouth and dropped his sandwich on his plate. "The fuck?"

My jaw clenched, and I narrowed my eyes at him. "Words, fuck stick. Speak."

"You've been hanging out with that waitress? You brought her donuts? And whose day did you make? Does she have a boyfriend?" Jon pinched the bridge of his nose. "I'm so confused."

"None of your business," I spoke through gritted teeth, and Jon reared his head back.

"I'll repeat—what the fuck? Are you fucking her?"

My brain hadn't fully processed his words before I was leaning over the table, grabbing a handful of his shirt and pulling his face close to mine. "Watch it. Watch your damn mouth."

Jon ripped my hand off his shirt and shoved me back. "What the hell is wrong with you?"

I looked around the diner, hoping like crazy that Grace hadn't seen all that. She'd hate that kind of attention. "She's my... friend." Jon's eyes looked like they were about to bug out of his head. I couldn't help but chuckle at his expression. "You're such an ass. I can have friends, you know. It is possible to be friends with a girl." My words weren't honest though. While Grace and I were starting a friendship, I wanted more. I knew I shouldn't, but I did.

Then again, I didn't think friends were supposed to make you hard as steel when they looked at and talked to you.

Jon took another bite of his burger and chewed slowly. "Okay." He swallowed before speaking. "You have a friend. Her name is Grace. You're *just friends*. What about that other part with the donuts and somebody else?"

I looked around again before answering. "She has a son."

"No shit," Jon yelled.

"Shut up," I whispered. "Yeah, she's a college student and a single mom. I met her kid, and he's a cool little dude." Jon continued to stare at me, so I went on. "I got them tickets in the family section to last Saturday's game. Then on Sunday I wanted to see if they had fun, so I brought them donuts. At the park. And we played together. You know, on the swings and shit."

Jon rubbed his hands over his face. "Did you just listen to your own words, Dean? Seriously?"

I sat staring at one of my best friends in the world, and I couldn't answer him. The fact that Jon would be shocked by the way I chose to spend my Sunday was not a surprise. I shocked the shit out of myself on that one. What bothered me was that his reaction was honest. I had never had girls that were friends. I'd never been unselfish enough to want that, and my best friend knew that about me. That sucked.

What seemed like a lifetime later, a plate of barbecue chicken, mashed potatoes, and green beans was placed in front of me. My stomach growled in anticipation. Grace placed a large glass next to it indicating it was sweet tea.

I looked up and couldn't help but smile. Her blush was back, this time creeping down her neck toward her chest. *How far down would that pink travel?* My gaze lingered on her breasts before I realized it and had to shake the thought out of my head. "Damn, Red. This is perfect. Thank you."

She nodded and looked over at Jon. "Can I get you anything

else?"

He stared at her for a long beat. "My friend here needs a lo-botomy. Can you help out with that?" Grace winced, and I kicked Jon's leg under the table. "What the hell?" he yelled, rub-bing his leg.

"We're good, thanks." I shrugged, hoping she'd think my friend was weird and not assuming he was talking about her. Me. Us. Finn.

Grace bit the bottom of her lip and left without another word. I took a bite of my food and groaned.

"What are you doing, man?" Jon pushed his plate away and leaned in.

I took another big bite. "Eating." Grace's choice was spot on. This was food like my ma made.

"You know what I mean. You're a whore. You're also a football beast. You're going to get drafted. And not like you don't know this already, but getting drafted means lots and lots of pussy." Jon's eyes glazed at the thought. "You know what does not get you lots of pussy?" He paused, and I kept eating. "Dating a single mom with a kid. That's insane." His last two words were loud, and then he smacked his hands on the table before he sat back.

I drank my sweet tea and glared at him. "We. Aren't. Da-ting." My best friend was pissing me the fuck off. "Just. Friends." I stabbed at the green beans like I'd like to stab at Jon's hand with my fork. "And why do you care?"

Jon grabbed his backpack and moved to leave the booth. He pulled out his wallet and threw money onto the table. Slinging one strap over his shoulder, he leaned over to my side. "'Cause my mom's a single mom. You grew up with June and Ward motherfucking Cleaver as parents. Me? I saw assholes skate in and out of my mom's life. They hurt her, and they hurt me. Fuck if my best friend will be one of those guys." My stomach dropped at his words, and I pushed my plate away.

"Do her a favor. Do the kid a favor. Hell, do me one. Stay away from a family that is obviously fragile. I love you, man, but you're a giant dick. You'll only end up hurting them." He turned and stormed out the door.

I scrubbed my hands down my face. *Holy shit, he's right.* Despite what I said to Grace, I couldn't stay friends with a girl that I was attracted to like I was with her. But what was the alternative? Grace wasn't a one-night stand type of girl, and I was so not looking for a relationship, least of all with someone who already had a child. I wasn't ready to be somebody's daddy. I was too young and too selfish for that.

I really was a dick. I didn't know Grace and Finn that well, but I knew they didn't deserve to be around a dick. I stood up and threw my money onto the pile on the table. As I reached down to grab my backpack, I saw Grace standing close by. Her face was pale, and as she dragged in a breath, she gave me a short nod. She'd heard. Everything. I didn't know what to say about that. I didn't know what I wanted anymore or if what I thought was right. I headed for the door, and when I turned back to tell her good-bye, she was gone.

chapter
Eight

Grace

I NEVER LEFT work for the day without some sort of food. Sylvie was a giver and loved to feed people. She wouldn't rest unless she knew that Finn and I had something home cooked for dinner. What I didn't know was that she was also a seamstress.

Finn jumped into Sylvie's open arms, wrapping his body around hers in a massive hug. "Miss Sylvie! Thank you so much!" Sylvie laughed and clapped her hands as Finn leaped across the room, his red, blue, and yellow superman bodysuit perfectly fitted, the shiny red cape flying behind him.

"Thank you." I kissed her soft, wrinkled cheek and watched tears fill her eyes. "Finn doesn't know his grandparents, and you've taken him on as if he were your own."

Sylvie wiped her eyes with a handkerchief. "I never married, never had kids. You and Finn are my family, Gracie."

Gracie. I didn't stop her from calling me that, but it killed me a little each time. My parents and Sylvie were the only people who called me Gracie. I missed my mom and dad. Almost five years had passed since we had spoken to each other. Before things went bad, we had been close. They had loved me and been proud of me, or so I thought. I didn't foresee us ever reconnecting, and that made a part of me ache.

Sylvie and I hugged good-bye, and then Finn and I left the restaurant, ready for trick-or-treating. Living in family housing on campus allowed life to feel more normal for Finn, but I knew very few of our neighbors would be answering the door for a trick-or-treater. Luckily Amy had invited us to come to her neighborhood.

As we walked across campus, Finn jumped on the brown and yellow leaves, crunching them under his gym shoes. My mind wandered to Dean. As hard as I had tried to avoid it, I kept thinking about him. I attempted to convince myself that I only thought about him because he was a hot guy. But for the past week, each time he'd crossed my mind, I focused on how he'd seemed to care about me and my life.

I'd heard his friend loud and clear. He wanted Dean to stay away from us. I was unsettled by the whole conversation. He was Dean's friend, and yet it sounded like he thought poorly of him. I couldn't ignore the fact that this stranger, Jon, wanted to protect my son and me from Dean, but I felt strangely defensive over Dean. In the short amount of time I'd spent with him, he was kind, funny, and polite. Why would Jon assume he would hurt us?

Everyone on campus knew about Dean's reputation with girls, but I'd never believed he was a bad person. He acted like a normal college student. I was the one who was different.

I was more bothered than I wanted to admit, however, about how he ended our *friendship*. As soon as Jon called him out, he walked away. No good-bye. No explanation. We hadn't spoken again, and he hadn't come back to Maria's to eat. Thank God I hadn't let Finn get close to him. As it was, I was going to have to explain that Dean was busy with football and unable to go to the park anymore. Finn would be disappointed, and that pissed me off.

"C'mon, Mama!" Finn tugged on my hand, and we crossed the street into Amy's neighborhood. The idyllic tree-lined road was filled with stone and brick homes, stately but not off-putting. Many faculty members lived in these homes and raised their families there. Amy stood on her front porch, which was decorated with mums and pumpkins, waving to us.

Finn jumped up and down, his orange plastic pumpkin banging against my legs. "Hello, Miss Amy!" Finn waved back. "You stay right there. Let me practice."

I stopped at the bottom of the stairs, and Finn ran up to Amy, holding out his pumpkin bucket. "Trick or treat, please!"

Amy laughed and held out a large purple bowl filled with miniature candies. Finn contemplated his choices carefully before selecting one.

"Are you ready to get that bucket filled with candy and fun stuff?" Amy placed the bowl inside her front door, and her mom waved good-bye from the kitchen.

Finn held on to Amy's hand and nodded.

"Thank you again for coming along with us." Amy and I walked side by side as Finn ran up to the house next door.

"I am excited to go. I have not been trick-or-treating in a long time." Amy pushed her pink glasses higher up on her face. She was a positive, joyful person. She told me almost every day how much she loved her job and how lucky she felt to have it. I, on the other hand, felt the children who learned from her were the lucky ones.

Ten houses later the pumpkin bucket was getting heavier, and Finn was walking slower. He was up later than normal, and if I pushed him too hard, he would get grumpy. "Finn, let's cross the street and head back. Once we get back to Amy's house, we'll be finished for the night."

"Okay," Finn nodded. As we crossed the street, a group of

college students moved past us, the girls dressed in very revealing costumes, the guys wearing jeans and T-shirts. They were a friendly group, yelling out "Happy Halloween" and complimenting Finn on his outfit.

"Grace?" I had recognized Dean's voice before I saw him. My heart raced, and my stomach twisted. "Hey, Just Finn! Wait, you aren't Finn. Is that Superman?" Dean turned and walked back to the sidewalk where we stopped.

"Yes, I am Superman!" Finn used a deep voice, and we all laughed when he puffed out his chest and placed his hands on his hips.

"Dean? Dean Goldsmith?" Amy moved from beside me and approached Dean.

"Amy! What are you doing here?" Dean and Amy hugged.

How in the world did those two know each other?

Amy twisted around and pointed to her house. "My Dad got a teaching job here. After Clemson, I moved here. I work at childcare on campus." She smiled down at Finn. "I help Finn."

"No way," Dean looked at Amy then at Finn and then at me. The look of remorse in his eyes made my chest tighten. "That's great news, Amy."

"Are you trick-or-treating?" Finn looked Dean up and down with his eyebrows pinched together. "What's your costume?"

Dean crouched down by Finn. "No, little dude. I'm heading to a party with some friends. I'm just dressed like me."

He didn't need a costume. Dean was so handsome he took my breath away. His long-sleeved T-shirt was tight, and the definition of the muscles on his chest and arms were clearly evident.

"Grace, can I talk to you for a minute?" Dean placed his hand on my arm, but I pulled it away. It was clear he regretted befriending Finn and me. I didn't want him to try and say something to make me feel better about it. What I wanted was to forget the whole thing.

I shuffled backward, finding Finn's hand and slipping my

own around it. "No, you can't. I'm going to finish trick-or-treating with Amy and my son. Have fun at your party." I turned and walked to the next house, pulling Finn along with me. He ran to the front door while Amy moved next to me. Looking over my shoulder, Dean stood still, hands clenched into fists and body slumped. He watched us with a pained expression on his face.

My stomach hurt, but I took a deep breath and looked back at Finn. *Finn*. He was my priority. No matter how nice Dean had been, or how he had made me feel, even for a minute, he was not the guy for me. I had one goal, one focus. I needed to graduate so that I could continue to take care of my child. A Dean-sized distraction was not what I needed.

As we walked to the next house, I chanced a look back in his direction, but he was gone. My heart sank just a bit further.

"He used to be an asshole," Amy looked off in the same direction, toward the party Dean was attending with his friends.

"How do you know him, Amy?" I glanced down at her, a little shocked by her comment. My eyes wandered over to Finn, who was still on the porch choosing his treats.

Amy looked over at Finn and smiled as she continued. "Dean went to my high school. I did not have classes with him. I was in special classes."

My mouth dropped open. No way. Amy and Dean went to school together? I wanted to pepper her with questions. I wanted to know what he was like, who he hung out with, and who he dated. But I kept my questions to myself.

We walked on, and Amy continued. "Remember I told you about Emma?"

I nodded. Emma Harris made such a huge impact on Amy's life during her senior year of high school. "Because of her, you went to Clemson. Because of Clemson, you get to work with Finn."

Amy grinned. "She's the best. You know I was her teacher's aide, but Dean was a student in her class senior year, along with his best friends Landon, Jon, and Ricky. She had a rough start. Dean ruled the school. Dated all the girls. Homecoming king, prom king, quarterback. And he was mean. Real mean. To me and to other kids. He gave Miss Harris a hard time."

I felt lightheaded. Jon was right. Dean was a dick. I needed to hear this. I wouldn't let Finn near him again.

"But you know what?" Amy took Finn's hand as we walked up the pathway to her house. "He changed, Grace. Landon fell in love with Miss Harris. They could not be together until graduation, but senior year he learned to be a good man. Dean did too. They both stuck up for kids like me. They were kinder. Landon even took me to the prom." Amy's face broke into a wide smile, and a lump formed in my throat.

"Amy, that's so special. I'd like to meet this Landon. Finn, choose some treats and let me check them out to make sure they're safe." Finn took a few minutes making his selections, and I inspected them carefully. Then he sat on the porch of Amy's house and devoured three miniature candies and a full-sized candy bar. "We're leaving in two minutes, buddy. You can polish off the rest of these tomorrow." Finn grinned, chocolate smeared all over his face.

"Landon is great, but he got that way because he met Miss Harris. She made him want to grow up and do the right thing. Dean got better watching them. He is not a bad guy anymore, Grace. Don't listen to what other people say. Trust me. I know."

I hugged Amy and whispered my thanks. Trusting what Amy said was easy. She had no ulterior motives. Amy only liked to make the people around her feel good. Knowing that Dean had changed in high school was one thing, but it didn't mean his world and my world had any reason to meet.

After saying our good-byes to Amy and her mom, we set off back to campus. Five minutes into our walk home, Finn slumped against me. "I'm so tired, Mama." I lifted him and his bucket of candy into my arms and walked toward our home. He fell sound asleep.

As I approached my apartment building, I spotted Dean sitting on the bench by the door. *Crap.* He was going to make me talk to him. I steeled myself to push him away, and then I remembered Amy's words. He wasn't a bad guy. And some part of me *had* missed his company.

He jogged my way as soon as he saw me. "Let me have him, Red," Dean scooped Finn from me before I could protest.

My arms ached, and I stretched them out in front of me. "Thank you. He's heavier than he looks." Dean only nodded, his face somber. We walked the rest of the way, and I held the door to my building open for Dean. We rode the elevator in silence, and when I unlocked the door to my apartment, he followed me inside.

"Should I lay him on his bed?" Dean whispered.

"No," I said as I rubbed Finn's arm. "I need to take him to the bathroom and brush his teeth. He ate a lot of candy." Finn woke up and smiled at Dean, face still covered in chocolate.

"I can see that. Hey, little dude."

Finn yawned. "I'm sleepy, Dean."

I helped Finn in the bathroom and then got him tucked in his bed. Shutting the door to his room, I walked into the living room. Dean sat on my couch, his elbows resting on his knees.

"I hope you don't mind that I came here, Red. I'd like to talk to you." Dean's voice was rough, and for some reason the lump was back in my throat. What was wrong with me around this guy?

I sat next to him on the couch. "It's okay. Why did you leave your party so early?"

He turned to face me. "I never went. I've tried, but I can't get you out of my head."

"Dean, you don't need to worry about me. Finn and I are fine. We've always been fine." My anger rushed to the surface, and I felt hot all over.

Dean placed his large hand on my knee. "I'm not thinking about Finn. I mean, he's great, of course, and I do think of him." Dean ran his other hand through his hair and blew out a breath. "I'm thinking about you. I'm serious. All day long I wonder what you're doing or what you're thinking about." Dean stood up and walked to the window, looking out into the dark sky. "My best friend was raised by a single mom. He wants me to stay away from you. He thinks you'll be another game to me." He didn't face me. He continued staring out the window.

I stood up and moved behind him. The heat from his body warmed mine, even without touching. His smell was fresh and clean with only a hint of cologne. "Am I?" My voice was whisper soft, and he turned around; one step closer and our bodies would touch. I willed him to take that step. "A game to you? Is that what this is? You said it's not pity or worry, so what is it?"

He took that step, his hand reaching to cup my jaw. My body tingled, charged with the nearness of him. "Attraction, Red. Not a game. Not pity. I don't feel bad for you. You're one of the toughest people I know. I want to know more. I want to be near you."

I whimpered.

As soon as the noise escaped from my lips, I closed my eyes. *Shut up, Grace.* So much time had passed since I'd allowed a man to get close enough to truly *want* me. I nearly forgot the power behind that sentiment.

My knees weakened, and I trembled. His hand remained on my face, and when he felt me tremble, heard my whimper, registered that my eyes were closed—he reacted.

I didn't see his lips come closer to mine, but I knew it was happening. Every other sense was magnified. I heard the sound of his breathing increase in speed. The smell of his cologne became intoxicating, and I felt the warmth of his chest as it pressed against me when he pulled me closer. Then his lips found mine, and he held them there, almost as if he was asking permission.

My eyes fluttered open and I shifted, fisting his shirt in my hands, holding him to me.

I opened my mouth, and our tongues met, sliding together, exploring and tasting. I released his shirt and brought my hands up and around his neck. A moan erupted, and it took a few seconds before I realized it came from me. Dean groaned in answer, running his hands down my sides and along my back.

Neither of us would break the kiss. We moved, Dean pulling on my lower lip, biting gently. I ran my tongue along the edge of his lips, teasing and coaxing them back open. Then our mouths were fused together. The kiss became desperate. We communicated words we had never spoken to the other through that kiss. This was real. This was different. I knew enough from what I was feeling to be scared, but I was still not willing to stop. I held myself back from climbing his body, the ache inside me growing like a wildfire.

"Grace." Dean pulled back, resting his forehead against mine as he gasped for air. "You feel that, right? It's not just me?"

I laughed softly, kissing the corner of his mouth. "I feel it."

He placed his hands on my hips, shifting me so he could look into my eyes. His blue eyes sparkled, and something inside me melted. "Let me get to know you. Let me in."

He already was in he just didn't know it. "Yes. I want to know you too."

Dean smiled, and it was like the sun broke through from the night sky. "Okay. Tomorrow can I come by after Finn goes to bed? I figure you need to be around me more before you're comfortable with me hanging with Finn. Maybe we could start by studying together?"

He sounded so unlike the Dean I imagined him to be. His voice and his demeanor were gentle. He was taking it slow, which I desperately needed, and he was allowing me to make the decisions that were right for my family.

I nodded, suddenly shy, which was silly considering I'd just kissed him with more passion than I knew existed inside of me.

His lips tilted up, and he kissed my lips softly. "Lock up behind me, Red."

And he was gone. Out the door and into the night but slowly making his way into my heart.

chapter
Nine

Dean

I HELD OFF until eight thirty before I knocked on the door. I'd waited all day for this. My body was keyed up, the anticipation of seeing her coursing through me. I had guessed—correctly, it seemed—that she wouldn't want Finn to see me over at her place right away. She would need to trust me before she let Finn spend more time with me.

I intended for exactly that to happen. I couldn't explain what was happening to me. I had never felt an attraction like this. In a strange way I was proud of her. I barely knew her, but I knew enough. She was doing it all. Grace was a mom, a student, she worked a job, and made a home for her family. She was so quiet and small and yet her strength was overpowering.

Some guys would say being interested in a girl with a kid didn't make much sense. For me, it wasn't an issue. Maybe because Grace and Finn were *real*. Grace wasn't fake like so many of the girls I "dated." Grace and Finn were honest and funny, and I found myself wanting to be near them—both of them.

My family was fucking awesome. Seeing this little family stirred something in me that I didn't know I wanted. A sense of protectiveness overwhelmed me. I needed to make sure nothing ever hurt her or Finn. Especially me. I would never hurt them.

Grace opened the door with a smile. "Hey." She let me in and then locked up behind me. Her hair hung free, falling down her back in waves. I'd never seen it down before, and I had the uncontrollable urge to wrap my hands in it and bring her close to me. She wore IU sweatpants and a long-sleeved white shirt. Brown-framed glasses sat on her nose. *Holy. Fuck.* I had never, in all of my twenty-one years, thought glasses looked sexy on a girl. But on Grace? My entire body thrummed from the sight of her, and I blew out a breath to try to calm myself down.

"How was your day?" I followed her to the couch and sat down next to where she had her laptop open and several books laid out. Running my palms along my jeans, I wiped away my sweat. Was I... nervous?

Grace's eyes softened at my question. She sat next to me, her fingers knotted together. "Good, thanks. The usual. Classes, work, picked up Finn. We ate, and he played for a while before bed." She turned to face me. "How was your day?"

It hit me that as much time as I spent with the opposite sex, I wasn't sure I'd ever checked on someone like this. I never wanted to know how their day had gone. Everything was different with Grace. "It was good." My words rumbled out of my chest, and I brought my thumb to her lip, running it across the bottom. Her lips opened, and she kissed my thumb.

My body jolted. She hadn't even used her tongue, and I was hard as a rock. "Grace," I pleaded. I couldn't study. Not yet. I had to taste her. I had to feel that connection again.

Grace slipped her glasses off her face and moved closer to me.

"You look sexy as hell in those glasses, Red." I moved even closer to her until I felt her breath wash over my face.

She wrinkled her nose and leaned back. "No way."

"Yes, way. But it's good you took them off." I cupped both hands around her face and lowered my head until our lips met. We started the kiss with tender movements, but when the fire raced through my blood, I was lost. I groaned, and she opened her mouth to me. Our tongues slid together, each meeting the other with matching ferocity. Our hands moved everywhere in an attempt to feel everything all at once. Hers moved from my arms to my hair, tangling in the strands, pulling me to her. Mine traveled from her face down to her hips, along her rib cage, her back, and then finally moving into those long strands of red hair, just like I had imagined.

"Mmmm," Grace moaned against my lips, and when I pulled back to look at her, my dick swelled at the sight of her swollen red lips. I pictured her lips on me, and I wanted to beat my chest and grunt.

We were both breathless, but I couldn't take my hands off her. I couldn't stop watching her, dark pink cheeks, the way her eyes were hooded. Her fingertips traced her lips, almost as if she wanted to feel them because they were plump from our rough kisses.

"I guess we better study, huh?" I chuckled, and Grace took a deep breath, putting her glasses back on her face.

"Sorry. I got carried away." Grace's voice was hesitant, and she looked down at her hands again.

I scooped her up onto my lap. "One thing I need you to do for me, Red." She waited, head cocked to the side. "Never feel embarrassed around me. Especially about wanting to touch me or kiss me." I shifted her back a little so that she would feel how much I wanted her.

Bingo.

Her eyes widened, and then her face flushed red. She closed her eyes and licked her lips. "Oh." She swallowed, and I considered moving her again so that she would be straddling me and could feel me even better. But that was too much for tonight. Grace needed me to behave and move slowly.

"You got me, Red?" I kissed her softly on the lips.

Grace opened her eyes and nodded. "Time to study, right?"

I moved her next to me, placing an arm around her shoulder. "What's your major?" I couldn't believe how little I knew about her. I wanted to know everything. Every little detail that made up her whole.

"Business. Yours?" She moved a book onto her lap and handed me a bottle of water.

I took a long drink before answering. "Marketing. I'm graduating this December, a semester early."

Grace opened her textbook and smiled. "Whoa. And here I pegged you for a dumb jock when we first met. Look at you, graduating early. How were you able to manage that along with playing football for a team like IU?"

I rubbed my thumb along the soft material on her shoulder. "I've taken summer classes since freshman year. I'm hoping to get drafted this spring, so I knew if I wanted to graduate with a degree, I'd need to do it early."

Grace's eyes widened. "Wow, the NFL. That's so exciting, Dean. Although after watching you play at that game, I understand why. You were fantastic."

"Thanks, Red," I grinned and opened my book.

Grace took a drink of water, and I watched her swallow. I wasn't going to get any studying done at this rate. I also didn't give a shit.

"Can I ask you a favor?" Grace asked.

"Of course." I moved to face her.

Grace marked her place in her text with a pencil and shut the book. "When I took Finn to the game to see you, he asked me all about football. I didn't know how to answer many of his questions. Would you teach me so that I can help him understand the game?"

Two things happened at the same time. My chest heated with the thought that I could help Grace and that she trusted me enough to ask me for this. My stomach sank, though, when I realized that if she was asking me for help, she couldn't or wouldn't ask Finn's dad.

"Grace, I'd be happy to do that. I can teach Finn the basics too if you want." I laced my fingers with hers. If I was going to get to know all of her, and if she was going to let me in, I had to continue. "You can't ask Finn's dad?"

Grace closed her eyes and inhaled a big breath, blowing it out slowly. "Dean, I'll tell you. I promise. This is mortifying to say to you because it solidifies my nerd status, but tonight is the best night I've had in so long... I can't right now. Okay?"

This was the best night she'd had in a long time? We just kissed. We were attempting to study together. Pain shot through my chest when I contemplated how tough Grace's life was, and how easy I had it. I wanted to make her feel better. I wanted to heal her and touch her and...

But I would wait. "Okay, Red." I kissed each corner of her mouth. "Then let me hold you tonight. When you're ready to talk, just know I'm here."

I meant every word. No matter where football took me, I wanted to be there for Grace. At the very least, as a friend. But after kissing her, I hoped it would be as a whole lot more than just friends.

"WHO WANTS PIZZA?" I walked into Grace's apartment carrying a liter of soda and three large pizza boxes. I'd eat at least one all by myself. Our team was leaving the next day for an away game in Maryland. I'd be gone for a few days, so when Grace invited me to join her and Finn for movie night, I was stoked.

"Pizza's my favorite food!" Finn shouted, and I shot Grace a wink.

"Your sweet mama told me that, Just Finn." I placed the boxes on the coffee table and leaned over to kiss Grace's cheek. "You good, Red?"

She blushed.

That woman made me hard from her damn blush. Also from speaking. Oh, and from kissing my thumb.

Okay, anything Grace did made me hard.

Grace nodded, a soft smile spreading across her face before she headed into the kitchen. She came back with plates, napkins, and cups.

"Do you like the *Minions* movie, Dean?" Finn held up a DVD. "Miss Sylvie gave me this one for my birthday!"

"I haven't seen it, but it looks cool. Put it in." I sat back on the sofa and flipped open the box of cheese pizza. "When's your birthday, little dude?"

"September twenty-second!" He jumped up and down. "I didn't have a party this year cause Mama is in school, but next year she will have a job, and I get a party! I want to have a pool party. No, a bouncy-house party. No, a football party." He stopped jumping and looked down at his feet. "Would you come if I have a football party?"

My stomach sank. If all went according to plan, I'd be at the height of football season in September. Living in the state of the team I would be playing for. A state that could be across the country. But damn, if I could, I'd be at that little dude's birthday party. Finn made me laugh. He was easy to be around, and he looked at me like I was… more. More than a football player or a college jock. Like I was a man that he respected. And hell, if I didn't like that. I think I *needed* that.

"I'll try, Just Finn. I'll try real hard." I handed out slices of pizza and avoided looking at Grace for a few minutes. Right now

I wanted to forget about the coming months and watch this movie with the strange little yellow men that Finn was so excited to watch with me.

TWO HOURS AND two pizzas later, Finn was asleep against Grace. The movie had ended, but Grace and I kept talking as the credits rolled in the background. I wanted to know every single thought in her head. And then I wanted her to put Finn to bed so I could kiss her.

Finn stirred and snuggled closer to Grace.

"What's your favorite thing about being a mom?" I entwined my fingers with hers and gave a gentle squeeze.

"Hmmm. That's a tough one." She looked down at her son and then up at me. "I would have to say it's watching him grow and change. What I never fully understood before him was that as he grew up, I would only love him more. He's my favorite person in the world."

For a second I felt jealous. *Grow the fuck up, Dean.*

I kissed the tip of her nose. "He's lucky to have you, Red. And I'm feeling pretty damn lucky myself right now."

Grace smiled, that shy little grin that I adored, and my pulse sped up. I could honestly say that I was the lucky one. With this girl and her boy, eating pizza, and watching a movie about minions.

I was exactly where I wanted to be.

chapter
Ten

Grace

WE WERE FALLING into a pattern. Dean came over every night after Finn went to bed. We kissed until my body throbbed, but he never pushed me for more. I could tell by his body's reaction that he was turned on by me, but was he being patient or was it something else? After all, I wasn't a normal co-ed. That was glaringly obvious as we forced ourselves to whisper and attempted to avoid tripping over toys.

I heard the light knock on my door, and my heart raced. Being around Dean was an experience for every part of my body. I loved listening to his jokes and hearing our laughs mingle. Seeing him, his tall, muscular body folded onto my couch made my skin warm. He had a unique smell, always coming from a workout or practice. His scent was clean, but with a hint of his cologne that was so masculine I wanted to bury my face in his neck and breathe. And then his touch. I melted when his hands touched me, his lips pressed against me, his tongue stroked me. I was lit from within, on edge, always needing more. But I was afraid to ask for more. My gut told me he wanted to keep this simple, and taking it too far would mean complications.

"Hey." I opened the door and stood on my tiptoes to hug him.

He dropped his bag and wrapped his arms around my waist. "Red." He buried his face in my hair, which I always wore down at night.

For him.

His lips found mine and tears pricked at the corners of my eyes. He already meant so much to me. He was tender and adoring, and I felt special around him. I felt... more.

"Mama?" We froze, wrapped in each other's arms. Finn's voice was shaky and scared.

I pulled away from Dean and went to kneel in front of him. "Baby boy, what's wrong?"

He sniffled, wiping his eyes. "I had a bad dream."

Dean came over and sat cross-legged on the floor next to us. "I hate bad dreams, little dude. What was yours about?"

Finn looked at Dean and modeled him, sitting cross-legged across from him. "A crocodile tried to eat my toes."

"That's terrible." Dean leaned forward. "What did you do?"

Finn's eyes went round. "I ran. Very fast. I'm speedy, you know."

Dean chuckled. "You are, little dude. I've seen you run. Lemme see your toes."

Finn stretched his legs out in front of him, and Dean counted them. "Ten. All there."

"What should I do if he comes back?" Finn looked back and forth between Dean and me.

"You know," I began. "I'm one hundred percent certain that was just a dream. Want to know how I know?" Dean and Finn both nodded, and I giggled. "We live in Indiana. We don't have any crocodiles in our state other than in the zoo. I listened to the news tonight. There have been no escapes from the zoo. You're safe, buddy."

Finn threw his arms around me in a hug and then did the same to Dean. As he pulled back, Dean took his hand in his. "Cool birthmark, Just Finn." He stared at the long brown birthmark on Finn's hand, close to his wrist.

"It's not a birthmark, Dean." Finn's face was serious.

Dean tilted his head to the side. "What is it?"

My stomach flipped. I knew what was coming. The conversation I had been putting off would happen tonight.

"An angel kiss. Mama said my daddy kissed my hand up in heaven to say good-bye to me before I came to see her here on earth." Finn pressed his lips to his angel kiss and then hopped up. "Night, night."

I blew him a kiss, and Dean waved as Finn walked back into his room. I joined Dean in his cross-legged position and faced him.

"I'm sorry I didn't tell you first." I took his hand in mine and studied the contrast. His large hand engulfed my small one, his tan fingers wrapped around my pale ones, which were dusted with freckles.

"Finn's father is dead?" Dean whispered, and I nodded. "How? Before he was born?"

I looked up into Dean's eyes, so crystal-clear blue they reminded me of the ocean. "His dad's name was Josh. He struggled with depression for a long time, and he died by suicide months before Finn was born." My voice cracked, and tears fell from my eyes, running down my cheeks. Dean pulled me onto his lap, rocking me back and forth, and kissed the top of my head.

"I'm so sorry, Grace." Dean's voice was raw, and my heart hammered in my chest. His knowing this was one more tie to him, one more link from my heart to his.

I looked up and brushed my lips against his. "I've always been on my own with Finn. He's never known any parent but me." I turned, straddling him, and placed my hands on his shoulders. "This doesn't change anything, Dean. Don't start feeling sorry for us. Finn and I are fine."

Dean closed his eyes and his jaw clenched and unclenched. When he opened his eyes again, his pupils were dilated, and his eyes flashed. "I don't feel sorry for you, Red. But I feel... a lot."

I stood up and held up one finger in pause. I walked into Finn's room and checked on him. Sound asleep. I closed his door and walked back to Dean, holding my hand out to him. He placed his in mine and jumped to his feet.

"I feel a lot too. Probably more than you can imagine. I feel more for you than I have for any other man, even though all we've done is kiss. Sometimes I wonder if you want... me? In that way? Or is it just that you feel sorry for me?"

Dean's eyes widened, and he growled, lifting me off my feet. I wrapped my legs around his waist. His body shook, and I linked my hands around his neck. "Which door is to your room?" he asked.

My pulse sped up. I hated admitting one more thing to him that he could pity me for. "I don't have a room."

He froze. I was certain he stopped breathing. He turned around, pressing my back against the wall. "This is a one bedroom?"

I looked down watching where our hips pressed together. "It's what I can afford."

"Where do you sleep, Red?" His voice was so rough I shivered.

"The couch. It's fine," I whispered.

"Where do you keep your clothes?" He sounded angry. I didn't want that either. No one but Sylvie knew or cared where I slept. Until now.

"In the hall closet. Some in Finn's room."

Dean blew out a long breath. "It's gonna take me some time to process all that you do for your son, Red. Just know that I know. And someday that kid will get it, and he will never forget how his mama gave all she had for him."

"Dean," I breathed out. "I'm fine." He stiffened, his arms tense around me. "But you haven't answered my question."

Dean changed direction and walked us over to the couch, laying me on my back.

"Do I want you?" His voice was raspy, and my pulse sped up. "All I do is think about you, Grace. I think about what you would look like underneath me, on top of me." He ran his nose along mine and then brought his lips to my ear. "I've never been a patient man. I've never wanted to be with a girl who deserved that patience. But for you, I'll wait. I'll wait until you're ready for me. 'Cause once I have you, Red, I'm not going to be able to stop."

Oh. Dear. God.

I licked my lips, and he groaned, pressing his lips to mine. My tongue met his, and we kissed. I sighed into his mouth. This was where I wanted to be.

He leaned over me, bracing himself on his elbows. His eyes searched mine. "How much are you ready for?"

I swallowed and ran my fingertips down his cheek. "I'm not ready for sex tonight. But…" I took a deep breath. "I want you to touch me."

Dean closed his eyes again and allowed his hips to fall between my legs that were cradling him.

Mother of God. He was so hard.

Dean pulled my T-shirt over my head. He reached behind his neck and pulled his off too. Then he lowered his body until our chests met. He rocked against me, and I shuddered.

"Oh, God. Dean, this feels… incredible." I gasped for air and raised my face toward his, sucking on his lower lip.

He chuckled. "I haven't even touched you yet, Red." He moved his head to my chest, and I froze.

Yes, yes, yes, please. Touch me. Touch me. Touch me.

He ran his nose along the swells of my breasts, and when he looked at me, his eyes were glazed.

I watched as his hand trailed closer to my bra. He reached behind me and released the clasp, still rocking his hips against me. Pleasure tore through my body, the ache in my core intensifying. *More. More. More.*

Dean pulled my bra off and threw it to the side. He cupped my breasts in his hands, running his thumbs over my nipples. I arched my back, holding my moan inside, desperate to stay quiet.

"Shit, Grace. I've dreamed of touching these. I wondered if you blushed here too." He licked one nipple and then took it in his mouth, sucking, while he rubbed the other. He'd know the answer to that question shortly. My body was on fire and my face, neck, and chest burned with heat. My hips rocked against Dean's, matching his rhythm, intensifying the connection between us.

"Mmmm." Dean had moved to the other nipple. "It's true. You even blush here. This creamy skin gets pink all over." He sucked, releasing my nipple with a pop. "Your body is sexy as fuck, Red. I want to kiss you, lick you, and suck you all over."

That did it.

"Oh, God. Yes, Dean." I moaned long and low as the orgasm hit me. The boy had dry humped the hell out of me, and it felt unreal. He held my body tightly to his until I stopped trembling. I kissed up his neck, pressing my lips to his jaw. "Thank you."

He laughed. "Don't thank me, baby. That was beautiful."

I buried my face against his neck. "*Shit.* Was I too loud?"

He kissed the top of my head and chuckled again. "No, you were perfect."

"It's been a long time, Dean. I'm sure you guessed that."

Dean sat up, holding me to him, and wrapped a blanket from the back of my couch around us. "How long?" His voice was flat, and his lips turned down in a frown.

"Five years." I looked away. I didn't want to see the shock or sadness on his face.

Dean's fingers drew my chin to him. "You haven't been with anyone since Josh?" I didn't see shock or sadness or pity. He almost looked relieved.

"I don't let guys come around Finn. You..." I smiled and played with a piece of his unruly blond hair. "You're different. You have been from the start." I tugged hard on a strand of his hair. "You know, all the stalking and creeper stuff. You won me over by pure stubbornness."

He chuckled and then drew in a large breath. "Thank you for trusting me." His hands crept back up to my breasts, circling them.

"So that was the first orgasm you've had in five years?" His chest puffed forward, and his grin was proud.

I ducked away again. "Well..."

He cleared his throat. "Well, what?"

"I can't tell you this." I tried to stand, but he pulled me back, tickling my rib cage and trapping me beneath him.

"You better tell me." He sucked on my neck, and when I didn't have to look in his eyes, I found it easier to say the words.

"We've—" I gasped. Shit, the ache was back. He sucked so hard, and it felt so good. "We've been doing a lot of kissing, and then you go home."

He stopped and drew in a jagged breath. "Grace," he groaned. "Please keep going. Please tell me."

I moaned as he moved to suck on my earlobe. "After you leave, I picture what you would do to me."

"Red, do you make yourself come?" His words were so hot in my ear that I clenched my legs together.

"Yes," I hissed, and he froze.

His eyes were black as night. All I could see were his pupils, and his big body trembled above me. "You lay right here, thinking of me and touching yourself at night?"

I bit my lip and nodded. No reason to lie to the man.

He released me from his arms, his head falling back against the couch. Dean pressed his palms to his eyes. "Fuuuucckkk."

As long as I was being brave, and most assuredly foolish, I sat up and cupped his groin, stroking and squeezing his hardness. "Have you ever done the same?"

He dropped his hands and winced, squeezing his eyes shut. "Three damn times a day, Red." He groaned as I applied more pressure to him. "But now that I've heard this, it'll be four."

I dragged my hand closer to the waist of his pants, and his eyes flew back open. Big bad Dean looked like he was in pain. Or was he holding back with all that he had? Unable to tear my eyes away from his face, I took in the tension I saw and then the pleasure as I released him from his athletic pants. He was hard, but his skin was smooth as silk. It had been a long time since I had touched a guy, and Josh had been a boy, not a man. I started slowly, moving my hand from root to tip and then increased my pressure and speed when Dean's breaths became heavy.

"Grace, you're perfect. Just like that, baby." His mouth hung open, and I panted, unable to get enough air, from the erotic view in front of me. "God, that feels so good. I want you so bad." He pressed his mouth together, suppressing his moan as he came. I slowed my strokes and kissed his chest, his neck, his jaw, and his lips.

Dean took my face in his hands and kissed me for a long time. His eyes were full of devotion, and his mouth worshiped mine.

There were no more words tonight. We had officially left the land of simple and were planted firmly in the world of complicated.

Funny thing was, I wouldn't have it any other way.

chapter
Eleven

Dean

JON TAPPED MY shoulder, and I opened my eyes. "What's up?" I asked as I pulled my earbuds out. We were on a bus, driving home from our game in Ohio. IU's upset win over Ohio State made ESPN's college halftime show. The left side of Coach K's mouth had lifted into the shape of a grin when he heard, but the moment I registered his happiness, it was gone.

"You decided to ignore what I asked and what Coach K demanded, huh?" Jon sat in the seat next to me, staring out the window.

"What are you talking about?" I looked down at my phone where I had been texting with Grace for the past hour.

"I asked you, for me, as your best *fucking* friend, to not get involved with a single mom. Coach K told you that football needed to come first. Before girls. Seems to me you're thinking with your second head," Jon said with a glare.

I pressed my first head back onto the seat behind me. *Damn.* I still wasn't ready to talk about Grace with Jon.

"I know I pissed you off." I turned to face him. "But give me a little credit, you know, as your best *fucking* friend, to not be like all the assholes your mom dated."

Jon crossed his arms over his chest. "You're not like those guys. I know that. But c'mon, man. Grace isn't just any girl. She has a child. A boy who I'm sure already thinks you're the shit. And facts are facts. You will be leaving Indiana to play football."

My phone dinged with an incoming text.

Grace: *Want to head over here tonight? We're making ice cream sundaes.*

Jon read the text over my shoulder. "Ice cream sundaes? You used to party all night after a game like we had today. This is what you want, man?"

I scrubbed my hand over my jaw. I didn't blame Jon for asking questions. I'd done a complete one-eighty in the past couple of weeks. Hell, I hadn't even had a hangover since I'd been spending all my free time with Grace. I was happy to choose ice cream over beer, and that surprised me. I could understand Jon's concern. "You said it yourself. She has a kid, Jon. That means ice cream on a Saturday night instead of shots of Patrón. I'm okay with that."

Jon studied me for a minute. "Does she know you'll be leaving soon? Does the kid?"

I texted her back before I answered him.

Me: *Sounds good*
Extra cherries for me
Anything red... :)

"We haven't discussed me moving, but she knows about the NFL. We'll work it out, Jon. We haven't made a formal commitment to each other. We're taking it slow."

"Coach K know about this?" Jon asked.

I half snorted. "Why should he? The only thing he asked is that I put football first. That's what I'm doing."

Jon didn't respond to that—he just stared out the window at the highway zooming past us for a few minutes. "I just don't get why you want to date a girl with a child."

"Full disclosure, it would be easier if Grace was not a mom. I'm not an idiot. Finn complicates her life and mine now that we're dating. But I like that little dude. I don't mind complicated either. Jon, I dig her. I dig both of them. And Finn is her whole world, so he'll be a big part of mine as long as we're together."

Jon turned from the window and glared at me. What the fuck was his problem? He couldn't let this go, and it was none of his goddamn business. He opened his mouth and then snapped it shut, focusing his attention back on the window and the world outside it.

I put my earbuds back in and closed my eyes. I tried to focus on football and replay the game in my head, but my thoughts kept drifting to Red and Finn and their ice cream sundaes waiting for me back home.

Two hours later I knocked on their door.

Red answered, a sexy smile on her face. "Congratulations. You played great today." She stood up on her tiptoes and kissed my lips.

I dropped my bag and wrapped my arms around her waist, lifting her off her feet. "All I could think about on the drive home was kissing your sweet mouth, right after you eat a bite of ice cream." I kissed along her jaw and up to her ear, lightly biting the lobe. She moaned, her grip on my arms tightening. "Your tongue will be cold and sweet, and I'm gonna suck on it."

Grace leaned back, her eyes dancing as they met mine. "I'm gonna hold you to that. But right now, we have company, bad boy."

Shit. I was all geared up. I eased her off me, difficult as I now had a raging hard-on.

"Dean!" Finn ran out of the kitchen holding an ice cream scoop and a jar of chocolate sauce. "You're here! Mama said we had to wait to eat until you came. I'm so proud of you. You threw that ball right to your guy. And then touchdown!" He held up his hand, and I high-fived him.

"Thanks, little dude. I'm starving after all that ball throwing. Let's make some sundaes." Finn dragged me into the kitchen to show me the row of sprinkles, whipped cream, and my favorite, cherries.

Grace opened the freezer and pulled out one container of vanilla and one of chocolate ice cream. She opened the lids and then placed the chocolate sauce in the microwave.

"Oh yes!" Finn giggled and clapped his hands. "This is such a treat. Mama only buys ice cream and toppings for real special times."

I looked sideways at Grace. She was busy pulling out bowls and spoons, organizing the assembly line and avoiding eye contact with me. I hadn't even thought about the cost of treats like these. This was a big splurge for Grace and Finn.

I bent down and focused on Finn. "What's the special occasion today, little dude?"

Finn's eyes sparkled with happiness. "You, silly! Mama tried to think of a way to celebrate your win. This was my idea! I just knew it would be the best party ever if we had ice cream sundaes waiting for you." He threw his arms around my neck and hugged me.

I stood up, holding him to me and turned to Grace. "This is all for me?"

She gave me a small smile. "You're probably used to wild parties after your game, and I'm sure our version of thirty-one flavors doesn't quite cut it. If you'd rather celebrate with your teammates, we understand. We just wanted to do something for you… from us."

Finn lifted his head off my shoulder. "From us!" He laughed and wiggled free. I set him down on the ground, and he grabbed a bowl. We stood at the counter, Grace doling out huge heaps of ice cream, piles of whipped cream, and thick warm spoonfuls of chocolate sauce. I added the cherries, placing three on the top of my sundae.

Finn sat down in his chair and ate. "Dean?" he asked, a dribble of chocolate on his upper lip. Grace leaned over and wiped it with a napkin. "Isn't this a great way to celebrate your big win?" He didn't wait for my answer, he just dove back into his dessert.

"It sure is, Just Finn," I answered him and then looked across the table at Grace.

She thought I'd rather celebrate with my teammates, and so did Jon. The thing was, a night of beer and Patrón had never made me feel like this.

I scooped a huge bite of ice cream and tapped my spoon against Finn's. "Cheers, little dude."

"Cheers." He giggled back.

We sat at Grace's table and ate together, the three of us, celebrating my win with the best ice cream sundaes I'd ever eaten.

WHEN YOU'VE KNOWN your friends your whole life, you form traditions with them, just like you do with your family. At Thanksgiving, tradition had been that the Goldsmiths had their holiday dinner at noon. Then I would meet my friends at the lake, we'd grab a few beers, and go to Landon's parents' house for their formal, catered Thanksgiving party.

Since Landon had pissed his parents off, both by falling in love and losing his scholarship to IU, we skipped the last part of the tradition. Now we would crash his girlfriend's home and eat a second dinner with her family.

What I hoped we never gave up was meeting at the lake. Today was freezing, and Jon, Ricky, and I were cold enough that we wore hats, jackets, and gloves. The gloves were mostly so we could hold our beer cans without getting frostbite.

"Where the fuck is pussy boy?" Jon leaned back against my truck, slamming his beer back.

Ricky laughed. "Land's on his way. Chill out."

I grabbed a beer and popped the tab. "I think he and Emma flew in late last night from Cali. They're probably beat."

We turned at the sound of gravel crunching. An old-as-shit Honda approached, and Landon jumped out of the driver's seat, hurrying over for one-armed man hugs and slaps on the back.

"Nice ride. Bet you're missing your truck back in Cali." I handed him a beer, and he rolled his eyes with a nod.

"Dean, watch it. My car isn't fancy like the trucks you boys have, but it works." Emma walked over with a smile and hugged each of us.

Emma was hot. That was undeniable. When she was hired to teach at our high school right out of college, we were stoked. Economics was much more fun when you looked at a gorgeous blonde with great knockers. What none of us ever anticipated was that she and our boy Landon had been hooking up all summer. Of course that was only because Landon had lied about his age, but still. Landon would always be a legend in our group.

Amy exited the backseat and walked over.

"Amy! Hey!" I hugged her, and Jon and Ricky waved. "I thought you were in Bloomington?"

Emma bent her head to the side and watched us. She was protective over Amy. She had been since she took her on as her teacher's aide. I thought it was cool as shit that they stayed friends even after Emma and Landon moved to California.

"My parents and I came home to be with the rest of our

family. My aunt and uncle are hosting dinner." She smiled and adjusted her glasses. "I am looking at apartments for next year. When my dad's job ends, we will move back home. I am going to share a place with some friends."

"That's sweet, Amy." Jon held up his beer can in acknowledgment, and Emma frowned. "Sorry, Ms. Harris."

"Ugh! Cut it out, Jon. You know damn well that I'm not your teacher anymore." She stomped her foot in frustration, and we laughed.

I turned back to Amy. "Will you work at another preschool?"

Emma narrowed her eyes. "Dean, how do you know where Amy works at IU?"

Amy giggled, holding her hand over her mouth. "You want to tell her or should I?"

I winked at Amy. "Nothing to hide, Ms. Harris." Emma punched my shoulder. "Ow." I rubbed it and continued. "I'm dating a senior at IU, who has a son. He's in Amy's class."

Amy nodded with a proud smile on her face. Jon frowned and popped open another beer. Landon stood behind Emma, wrapping his arms around her shoulders. They spoke at the same time.

"You're dating?" Landon asked mouth agape.

"You're dating someone with a child?" Emma screeched.

Ricky hooted. "We're all thinking the same thing. You're still a damn kid yourself, Dean."

I saluted Ricky with my middle finger. "Settle down. Grace is awesome, and so is Finn. She's a fantastic mom. She goes to school full time, works at Maria's Diner, and raises Finn. Yeah, we're dating. So what?"

Landon still hadn't shut his damn mouth, but Emma's face had softened into a grin. Jon stepped forward, pointing at me. "You know what the problem is. You'll leave them. And when you do, you'll hurt her, but more importantly, you'll also be hurting that kid."

An awkward silence surrounded us.

"You are not going to hurt them, right Dean?" Amy's face was contorted in confusion.

Shitballs.

"No, Amy. I'm not." I glared at Jon, and he rolled his eyes and leaned back against my truck.

"Is this serious, man?" Landon asked and took a drink of his beer.

I frowned. Yes, it was serious. But it wasn't Emma and Landon serious. We weren't in love. We weren't moving away together. I cared about her and Finn, but things were still new with us. I wasn't sure how to answer.

"Getting there." I kicked at a rock with my boot. "I really like her. And Finn too."

"Is there a dad in the picture?" Emma asked quietly. She had told me last year that she had no relationship with her father, so this was a real soft spot for her.

My lips pursed before I answered. "No." They didn't need to know the details.

Amy rubbed her mittened hands together. "I feel sad for them today."

I stopped breathing and took a step forward. "Why, Amy?" I had spoken to Grace on the phone this morning. She sounded quiet, but fine.

Amy's eyebrows pinched together. "You know why. 'Cause they are alone."

I looked at my friends, my mind racing. Jon straightened and glared back. Emma and Landon exchanged worried glances. "She told me this morning she was getting ready for Thanksgiving dinner with her family."

Amy touched the base of her neck and paused. "Oh no. Maybe I should not have said anything. I am sorry." She looked at Emma, and Emma walked over, wrapping her arm around

Amy's shoulder.

"I think you need to tell Dean what you know, Amy." Emma looked down at her friend and then at me. Pity. She had pity in her eyes. "Dean cares about Grace and Finn, so if they're sad, he'll want to know."

Amy nodded. "I do not know why, Dean, but Grace has no family but Finn. She never sees her parents. I know she and Finn are alone on all the holidays. Finn told me one time at school. He cried and asked Santa to bring him a family. Last year all he asked for was a daddy and a grandma and grandpa with white hair." Amy's chin wobbled at the end.

My heart slammed in my chest. "FUCK!" I roared, slamming my beer can down on the ground.

Amy jumped, and Emma hugged her. "You did the right thing saying something, Amy."

Landon stepped forward. "What're you gonna do?"

I reached into my pocket and grabbed my keys. Thank God I'd only had one beer. "What am I gonna do? I'm gonna go be with them!" I shouted, running to my truck.

"Drive safe!" Emma yelled, and as I passed, Landon squeezed my shoulder. His silent nod made my chest tighten.

I was going to take care of my girl and her boy.

BLOOMINGTON WAS ONLY sixty miles away, and that was a good thing. The campus was dead with everyone gone for the holiday, so I parked close to Grace's building. The smell of turkey filled the hallway, and I stopped to catch my breath before knocking on her door. I didn't want to scare her, but I was feeling out of control. I was devastated that she and Finn were alone. I was destroyed she hadn't trusted me enough to tell me this. And I was furious that I didn't know how to fix the problem.

I knocked on the door. I heard Finn call to his mom and her ask him to wait. Then the door opened, and there she was.

She took my breath away. She was dressed simply, in jeans and a gray sweater, her hair piled on her head in a messy bun, and her brown glasses on her face. Beautiful. *Perfect.*

"Dean," she gasped and immediately blushed. As overwhelmed as I felt, I couldn't hold back a smile. Her skin turning pink or red was one of the most adorable things in the whole damn world.

"Can I come in?" I asked, and she opened the door wide.

"Dean!" Finn ran over and wrapped his body around one of my legs. "Mama! We have company for turkey dinner!"

I swallowed against the rock in my throat. Why was life so fucking unfair sometimes? I looked up into Grace's eyes. They shone with tears behind her glasses.

I grabbed on to her hand and squeezed. "You have room for one more at the table?"

She choked back a sob and nodded. "Of course." I enveloped her in a hug, and she wrapped her arms around my neck.

I moved my mouth to her ear. "You and I need to talk later, okay?" I felt her head nod, but she didn't speak, nor did she let go.

I didn't want to let go either.

"WHAT'S YOUR FAVORITE food to eat at Thanksgiving?" I asked Finn as Grace sliced the pumpkin pie. Her dinner was nothing like the one my family had. My mom cooked for days, and she fed thirty people. Grace had cooked a turkey breast, mashed potatoes, green bean casserole, stuffing, and a pumpkin pie. Everything was from scratch and completely delicious, but it was simple. Instead of a prayer, Grace had asked us each to say what we were grateful for.

"My mama. She loves me and feeds my belly." Finn proclaimed.

I cleared my throat. "I'm grateful to be here with both of you." I looked at Finn first and then at Grace, hoping she could see how much I meant those words.

Grace took a sip of the wine I ran out and bought right before dinner. I used the excuse that my mom would never let me join another family for dinner empty-handed, but I wanted to make Grace's dinner special for her. She took care of Finn, but who took care of her?

"I'm grateful that I followed my heart." She looked at Finn and then at me. "Even when it was scary, I always listened to my heart." She wiped at her eyes and took another sip of wine. I held her hand under the table until Finn yelled out that he needed his turkey cut.

"I like mashed taters. Oh, and pie with whipped cream. Oh, and sparkly juice too!" Grace placed a slice of pie in front of each of us and grabbed a can of whipped cream from her fridge.

"Nobody let me drink this fancy-schmancy sparkling apple juice when I was a kid. I had to drink milk. What a bummer," I said as I grinned at Finn. Finn had told me that he and Grace shared sparkling cider on holidays to be fancy.

"Schmancy." Finn chortled. "That's funny!"

Grace approached Finn with the whipped cream. She sprayed a large dollop on his pie. "Open up!" She winked at me, and I watched her spray a mound into Finn's mouth and a tiny drop on the tip of his nose.

Finn giggled uncontrollably as he swallowed his extra treat.

"We've started our own traditions," Grace explained. "Want some?" She laughed and pointed the can to my mouth. "Or should I save it for later?" She winked and bit her bottom lip.

And... I was hard. I pulled her onto my lap. "Just on the pie for now, Red." I kissed her neck, and Grace shivered.

I was ready for later.
Right now.

chapter
Twelve

Grace

I SANG LULLABIES to Finn as I bathed him and put him to bed. I hadn't seen my son this happy in a long time. He had never known a holiday with anyone other than me, and having Dean present meant the world to him. My heart hurt when I thought of Christmas, Easter, or next Thanksgiving when it would be just the two of us again.

Walking back into the kitchen, I saw that Dean had ignored my direction to leave the dishes and had almost finished cleaning up from the entire meal. I wrapped my arms around his back and kissed between his shoulder blades before pressing the side of my face against him. I hummed, a sound of contentment, and Dean stiffened.

"That feels way too good, Red. You better cut that out." He turned around, moving me into his arms. "I have some pots and pans left to clean."

I reached up to kiss his lips. "I told you not to do the dishes." I scowled, and he tweaked my nose.

"At my house growing up, the girls cooked and the guys cleaned. Every holiday. Seems fair to me." Dean brought his mouth to mine, fusing our lips together. Then he swung me around, sitting my butt on the kitchen counter.

"Why didn't you tell me you and Finn were alone?"

I closed my eyes. My head felt dizzy and hot at the thought of what I had to tell him. "Kiss me first?" I whispered and opened my eyes. "I'll tell you my whole story, but first I need to be kissed."

Dean's eyes darkened. He ran his hand up my neck and into the back of my hair. I tilted my chin up, and he pressed his lips to mine. My mouth opened, and I traced the edge of my tongue along the seam of his lips. His mouth opened to me, and I tasted him, sucking on his tongue. We both moaned, and I wrapped my legs around his waist, trying to get even closer. My hands moved up his chest and around his neck.

Dean pulled away and dragged his mouth to my neck, kissing and sucking my skin along the way. "The things I want to do to you, Red." He bit my earlobe, and I moved my hips closer, rubbing against him. He groaned at the contact. My body was hot and needy and vibrating with lust for this man. "But we need to talk. Let me in. Let me know you."

I nodded, my eyelids heavy from my own desire. He lifted me off the counter and carried me into the living room. Dean sat on the couch, keeping me straddling him. He sat back and studied my face.

It was time.

"Josh was my high school boyfriend. He's the only guy I ever dated." Dean nodded and laced my fingers with his. "We slept together for the first time in the fall of our senior year of high school. Josh was depressed. He would go through bouts of pretty severe depression."

Dean's eyebrows pinched together. "What do you mean?"

"At first it was little things, like always finding the fault in situations. You know? He always saw the glass half empty to my half full. But then he'd get angry that I would see the good in situations."

Dean swallowed before asking, "Did he ever... hurt you?"

I placed my hand on my breastbone and could feel my racing heart. "Not physically. But emotionally he was a tough guy to love. Quick to anger, slow to reason with, and often despondent. As a teenager I didn't realize he was depressed. I thought it was me and that I bothered him or irritated him. So I was always trying to be better. More resilient. More loving."

Dean leaned forward and kissed my forehead. "Red, no one should ever make you, of all people, feel like you need to be more *anything*."

I smiled at him, and tears formed at the corners of my eyes. "My family is very religious. Ultraconservative. I promised my parents, my dad in particular, that I would never have sex before marriage." The tears welled up in my eyes and traveled down my cheeks. "But Josh wouldn't stop asking. He told me it would prove my love to him."

Dean unlaced our fingers and used his thumbs to brush away my tears. He didn't say anything, but his big blue eyes were full of sorrow.

"So we had sex. It wasn't good, but it pleased Josh. He seemed more... settled." I took a shaky breath and moved off Dean's lap. I sat next to him, wrapping my arms around my legs and resting my chin on my knees.

Dean's jaw was clenched tightly, but he allowed me my space. "I discovered I was pregnant in February." I closed my eyes and let the emotions of that time wash over me. The fear and confusion had left me paralyzed.

"What happened when you told him?" Dean spoke through gritted teeth. His body was taut, and his hands were in fists at his sides.

I opened my eyes. "That's the weirdest part, Dean. I asked

him to meet me at my house, and when I told him, I expected him to freak out. I expected him to yell or to cry or to blame me. But he didn't." I pressed my lips in a firm line and inhaled a long breath through my nose. "He calmly stated that he would have to stay home from college and get a job. He said his parents would be devastated and furious with him. But that was it. Then he left." I swallowed back a sob, and Dean pulled me, curled in a ball, back onto his lap.

"And then?"

I looked into Dean's eyes and spoke the hardest words I'd ever had to say. "He went home and shot himself with his dad's handgun. No note, no explanation."

"I'm so sorry, Grace. I'm so, so, sorry," Dean whispered as he kissed the top of my head.

I got up from his lap and walked over to the window. I took some deep breaths before I could go on. "I think it was the pressure and the realization that he had let his family down. I think that and the ongoing depression were what made him snap." I looked over my shoulder, and Dean sat with his elbows on his knees, hands clasped together, watching me.

"Whatever it was that made him take his life, I don't believe he knew how much pain he'd leave behind. His parents lost their child, and his child lost his father. And me?" My throat tightened from the pressure of holding back my sobs. "I'll never forgive myself."

"Forgive yourself for what?"

I kept my back to him, shielding him from the tears that ran down my face. "For getting pregnant. He didn't need any extra pressure from me. I should have told him he could go on to school and I'd handle everything. I should have told his parents so they could watch out for him. I should have... saved him."

Dean jumped up and walked over to me, placing his hands on my shoulders. "Grace, this is not your fault. Mental illness is a disease. It's not something Josh had control over, and it's sure as hell not something you could have prevented. Especially not as a teenager."

I wiped my tears away and then turned to face him. I wanted to believe what he said, but the guilt was too strong.

"I still don't understand why you're alone, Red. It sounds like Finn has two sets of grandparents." Dean asked in a low and wary voice.

My responding laugh was hard. "He does. But they want nothing to do with either of us."

He gripped my hands in his, voice trembling. "What the fuck do you mean?"

"I had to tell Josh's parents that I was pregnant right away. They were searching for answers and... well... I knew that was the catalyst for his actions." I looked at the floor, my shame keeping me from meeting Dean's eyes. "They blamed me completely. His mom told me I was a whore and that I had tempted Josh into sin, and his guilt caused him to kill himself. They said my baby was evil and the reason for the death of their son." Tears streamed down my face in rivers. I clasped my hand over my mouth as my stomach roiled. For a moment I thought I might get sick.

Dean walked away from me. This was too much for him. He didn't need to be burdened with my past. I sobbed into my hand, and when he turned around, his eyes blazed with heat. He engulfed me in his arms, his lips right near my ear. "I want to kick somebody's ass, Red. I'm holding back with every part of me to keep from losing it right now. Those people are the worst kind of motherfuckers. I get that they were grieving, but blaming you? Blaming... Finn? No wonder you can't let your guilt go." His voice cracked, and he pressed my body against his.

We held each other for a few minutes until our breathing slowed. "I'm scared to fucking death to even ask this, but what about your parents?"

I pulled back. Dean's eyes were red as they darted back and

forth between mine. "I told you before that my parents were religious, right?" He nodded. "They demanded my celibacy. So when I broke that promise, I broke their hearts. They told me that." Dean closed his eyes, and I watched his Adam's apple bob as he swallowed. "Most shocking of all was their insistence that I have an abortion."

Dean reared back. "The fuck?"

I nodded. My nausea continued, and my head throbbed. Sweat coated my palms, and I rubbed them on the legs of my jeans. "They were mortified that I would bring shame to them and to our church. They told me to get an abortion and then to repent for my sins. My mom even suggested I leave the country and do mission work."

Dean stared at me, and I watched the blaze in his eyes turn to ice.

"Of course I refused to have an abortion. I loved my baby from the moment I knew he or she existed. I also felt that my child was the last piece of Josh I had. As mad as I was with him for leaving us, I would never kill our child. I turned eighteen and graduated from high school in May, which made me a legal adult. I outright refused an abortion, and so they threw me out. My parents told me they never wanted to see me again."

Dean's face contorted. I felt the need to comfort him. I had had more than four years to accept my story. I had moved on.

I had Finn.

I grabbed Dean's hands and held them in my own. His big body shook. I wasn't sure if it was from anger, sadness, or both, but seeing him absorb my pain left me weak in the knees.

"You don't have siblings? Aunts or uncles that you could go to? Grandparents?" he asked.

I shrugged. "Josh and I were only children. My grandparents died years ago, and I'm not close to any aunts or uncles. It was just me."

"How did you? What did you? Fuck, Red. I've got to sit

down." Dean walked over to the couch, and I went back to the kitchen, returning with the wine bottle and our two glasses. I re-filled both and handed him one.

He took a long drink. "I'm not really a wine guy. I drink a fuck lotta beer though." I laughed, and his face relaxed. "This stuff's not half bad."

I sipped my wine and nodded. "I can't afford to buy any al-cohol, so this is a treat. I'm not going to lie—it's real helpful to have wine to drink when I'm telling this story."

Dean took a deep breath and then another long drink before placing his glass on the coffee table. "What happened after they kicked you out?"

"I took charge of my life. I had no choice. I packed up my stuff and took a bus to IU. As soon as I got here, I met with the Dean of Undergraduate Affairs and explained my story. It helped that I already had a full ride to IU on a business scholarship. I was able to change my living arrangements and get this apart-ment in the family-housing section of campus."

Dean held one of my hands in between both of his. "I didn't know there was a family section until I met you."

"There aren't many students with babies here, but at least there was a place for us to go. This apartment building is also open year-round, so for a small fee I could stay in the summer. The Dean helped me apply for placement at IU's Early Child-hood Center for daycare as well. I was due in late September, so we figured out that I could take a few online courses during my fall semester so that I could qualify for housing. Finn started daycare in the spring, and I returned to school full time. It's tak-en me an extra year to get enough credits, but I'll graduate this May." My chin tilted up, and I smiled. I was damn proud of that fact. I would graduate, and I would be able to take care of my son.

"Holy shit." Dean sat back on the couch and whistled. "Girl, I knew you were something, but hell, Red. That is the most amazing thing I've ever heard." He leaned forward and cupped his hands around my face, kissing the corners of my lips and resting his forehead against mine. "You're the strongest person I know."

Those dang tears were back, pricking at my eyes.

"How have you gotten the money you needed? Loans?" Dean's voice was soft. He rubbed his nose on mine, and my body lit up. I was drained from telling my story, but I needed the contact and connection that only Dean gave me.

"Mmm-hmm. I have a small student loan for emergencies. Mostly I get money for daycare and expenses from working at Maria's." I pulled back and asked, "Have you met Sylvie?"

Dean laughed, his eyes crinkling at the corners. "Umm, yes. She told me to stay the hell away from you."

"She's overprotective." I giggled. "She owns Maria's. I applied for a job there as soon as I put my boxes down in my apartment. Sylvie took me under her wing. She has always arranged my work schedule around my classes. She shopped with me at thrift stores for baby stuff and clothes. She's even babysat Finn for me." I smiled and played with Dean's long fingers, tangling them with my small ones.

He was quiet for a moment, and then he narrowed his eyes. "Was she with you when Finn was born?"

I held my breath for a second. "No. I was alone. But then I had Finn, and I was never alone again."

Dean closed his eyes and breathed out a curse. "I'm sorry you were by yourself when Finn came into the world. But I'm happy you've had a friend like Sylvie."

"Sylvie has been a true godsend. She sends me home with food every day. We would never have made it without her." I raised our entwined hands and kissed the back of Dean's hand.

He stiffened. "I've seen you leaving with a big bag. That's your and Finn's food?" He swallowed hard, and I frowned.

"Don't start feeling sorry for me, Dean. The point is we've

made it. Finn and I have made it all by ourselves. And with Sylvie's help. Heck, she'd be here for holiday dinners too, but she goes to visit her sister, Maria, in Florida." I smiled and rubbed my finger along Dean's furrowed eyebrow. "Stop worrying. We're fine."

Dean growled and flipped me onto my back, his hands behind my head to cradle me. "You gotta stop saying 'fine.' I get it, Red. I get that you're taking care of yourself and Finn. But you gotta know what hearing all this does to me. I don't want you to just be *fine*. I want to hurt people, make them pay for what they've said to you. I want to shake the shit out of anyone who missed the chance to see you as a mom and to love that little dude." He kissed along my jaw and up my cheek, over to my mouth. "Mostly, though, I want to kiss you all over and show you how much more than *fine* I think you are."

I took off my now smudged-with-tears glasses and put them on the table next to the wine. "Mmmmm, follow your instincts, football god. Let's go with the last option. Kiss away."

Dean chuckled and brought his mouth to mine, our tongues twisting and tangling together. We kissed and kissed, stopping to suck on a lip or neck only so we could catch our breath.

"Dean." I threw my head back, giving him unfettered access to my neck. His tongue dragged up, and my core clenched. I was trembling again but this time with desire.

"Hmm?" Dean murmured into my skin, and I laughed. He picked up his head, and his eyes twinkled. I was so glad to see the anger had melted from them.

I dragged my hands through his sandy-blond hair, and he placed his chin on my chest, looking up at me. "I want you to spend the night with me." Dean jolted and sat up. I moved and sat cross-legged next to him. "But not tonight. I'm not sure where we'd sleep. The couch is too small." I laughed, but Dean's face was stone at the reminder of my bed. I kissed his lips and stroked his jaw. "I also need to talk to Finn and tell him that we're dating. I mean... are we? Dating? I didn't mean to pressure you—"

Dean cut me off with a kiss so deep my toes curled. "Fuck, yes. To it all. I want to date, but I want more. I want you to be my girl. I mean I already feel like you are. Jesus." Dean ran a hand through his hair and chuckled. "I've always been kind of smooth around the ladies, Red. Just ask my buddies." He cupped my face with one hand. "But around you, I'm lost. I can't find the right words, and I feel like an idiot."

I opened my mouth to argue his point, but he stopped me with another kiss. "Talk to Finn when you're ready. I'll spend the night the minute you think it's a good idea. You lead here, Red. I'll follow." He bit my bottom lip and pulled it out, sucking it into his mouth before letting it go. "In this instance. But in other ways—" He dragged his other hand down, lightly skimming my breast. "I'm in charge."

chapter
Thirteen

Dean

GRACE SHUDDERED, AND her eyes fluttered closed. She licked her lips and nodded. "Yes."

"Grace?" My voice was rough, and my dick was as hard as steel. She opened her eyes, and her lips parted slightly. "I won't spend the night, but I want to make you feel good before I go."

Grace's face flushed, and she gave me a small smile. "Hold on one minute." She stood up and ran to Finn's room. I took the time to get myself the fuck together.

I had never in all my years heard anything like I heard tonight. Grace was the most special person I had ever known. I felt like a beast had been unleashed inside my body. Like King Fucking Kong, I would trample anyone who ever tried to hurt her again. I wanted to scoop her little body into my arms and care for her. I brought my fist to my mouth. This was so foreign to me—caring about a girl, protecting a girl.

And protecting a little dude too.

I looked up and saw Grace standing in front of me. She unwrapped her bun and let her long hair hang free down her back. My breathing stopped as she pulled off her sweater, leaving her in only a small lace bra and jeans.

"Holy fuck, Red." My dick swelled even harder, and I had to adjust myself as I stood up. Her little giggle made me smile. Seeing Red happy, especially after what she just told me, was fucking fantastic.

I stood in front of her and pulled off my shirt. My chest heaved as I watched the creamy skin on her neck and chest turn pink. She wanted me as much as I wanted her.

Grace reached behind her and unclasped her bra. Her beautiful breasts were bared to me, and I couldn't stop myself from reaching forward and cupping them in my hands.

"Dean," Grace gasped, and I lowered my mouth, sucking on each nipple. Her hands shot out and held on to my arms, clutching me as she threw her head back with a long sigh.

I placed kisses down her chest, down her belly, stopping at the button of her jeans. I raised my head, and she nodded, her breaths coming faster and faster. I unclasped her jeans and pushed them down and off her legs. Sitting back on my heels, I took in the sight of her tiny white lace underwear.

"Jesus. You're gorgeous." She closed her eyes, and I kissed her hips and then lower, on top of her panties, and she moaned.

"I have to sit, Dean. I'm going to fall. I want you so much I'm shaking." Grace's breathy voice was going to be the end of me. I stood up and scooped her into my arms.

I lay her on the sofa and pulled that little scrap of lace down and off her legs. She raised up on her elbows to watch me. I dragged my fingers down her, and she bit her lip. Watching her watching me was the hottest thing I'd ever seen. If I wasn't real careful, I was absolutely going to come in my pants.

I rubbed my fingers around her in circles and then slipped one inside. Her back arched off the couch with a low moan. "Dean…" She breathed out, and I placed my palm on her hip to hold her steady.

When I brought my lips to her and sucked, her whole body went rigid. I looked up, and her eyes were half-lidded, her breathing rapid.

"Oh my God. Yes, Dean. Oh, God yes." My fingers continued their movements, and my tongue circled, my entire fixation on bringing this woman pleasure.

Her hands found my hair, and she held on to my head as her eyes closed and her mouth dropped open in a long, guttural moan. Her body thrashed as she came, and I held her, slowly touching and stroking until she calmed.

When she opened her eyes, drowsy with lust, I sat back and took her in. She was a goddess. I wanted to treasure her. Bringing a woman pleasure and expecting nothing in return was something I had never experienced. Until her.

Grace crawled into my lap, her naked body wrapped around mine. "Dean? I don't know what to say. Nobody has ever... done that... and I... I really, really..." She looked up and giggled. "I mean, I really liked that." She ran her fingers up my neck and into my hair. "Let me take care of you too."

I held her tighter to me and pulled the blanket off the back of the couch, wrapping it around the two of us. "Not tonight, baby. Soon, I promise."

She lifted her head, and her eyebrows pinched together. "Why? I want to make you feel good."

I gently pressed her head back against my chest and ran my hands down her hair. "Grace, I'm not sure how to say this right, but I'm gonna try." I kissed the top of her head, and her body relaxed against me. "I listened tonight to your pain, and your struggle, and your love. And what I needed to do was to take care of you and you alone. Nothing for me. Just for you. 'Cause, Red? Nobody's done that for you in your whole life."

She looked up at me, tears filling up those beautiful green eyes. She'd shed enough tears for a lifetime. The time had come for someone to have her back and to take care of her.

"Until now. Until me. I'm going to keep on taking care of you because nobody has ever deserved it more than you."

I kissed her lips and held her to me. I'd leave in a little while and make it to my apartment before the sun was up.

And then I'd be back in the morning with donuts. All their favorites.

Because these two people had quickly become mine.

chapter
Fourteen

Grace

"SIT DOWN GIRL, and have some pie." Sylvie motioned for me to join her at the booth by the front door. The diner was empty, lunch rush over, and I had a few hours before I needed to pick up Finn.

I sat down across from her, and she poured me a cup of coffee. I sipped and rested my chin on my hand.

"How are you?" Sylvie cut a huge piece of cherry pie and placed it on a plate.

My chest warmed. Anytime we weren't busy, Sylvie made me rest and checked up on me. She treated me like a daughter, and I loved that about her.

I needed that from her.

"I'm good, Sylvie." I forked a bite of cherry pie into my mouth and moaned. Sylvie's pies were heavenly.

Sylvie sipped her black coffee, eyes narrowed in my direction. "What's going on with that boy? The tall blond? Kind of obnoxious?"

I laughed and wiped my mouth with a napkin. "I thought Dean was obnoxious too for a while. But he's... not. He's... special." I wanted to say more, but that might be rushing things. She would worry more than she normally did, and I never wanted that.

Sylvie pursed her lips. "I bet he's special, girl. That's what worries me. Is he special all over town?"

I smiled and nodded. "I know. I worried about that too. But I don't think so. I don't know why, but he seems to like... *me*." I emphasized the last word like it was a foreign concept.

Sylvie's head jerked. "Of course he likes you. Grace, you're one of a kind. There's nobody like you. I see the other girls your age, gigglin' like fools, drinkin' beer, and spendin' their daddies' money. Not you. Hard workin', lovin' your son, takin' care of your business. He'd be a fool not to see that and want someone like you in his life."

I swallowed hard. I thanked God every day for bringing Sylvie into my life. "I don't know..."

Sylvie took another sip of coffee. "What don't you know? What are you worried about?"

I paused. Looking out the front window, I saw college students, my age, who were carefree. I was not. "All those good things you said about me are also the things I worry about. Dean will probably become a professional football player. He will be able to have fun and date beautiful girls who have no responsibility tying them down. I wouldn't want their lives. I know what joy Finn brings to mine, but I worry that Dean will want that one day, or even worse, regret that he gave that up."

Sylvie nodded and placed her small hand, wrinkled from years of hard work, over mine. "No guessing what that boy is thinking. But you tell him what worries you, and let him decide. If he's got a lick of sense in him, he'll know there is no greater gift than you and your son." Her smile was shaky, and she cleared her throat. "Break's over. Customers at table five."

I stood up and leaned over her side of the booth, hugging her. "Thanks for the pie." She waved me off.

I wanted to thank her for everything she did for me, but that would make her uncomfortable. So I did what she needed. I took orders and kept her customers happy. But as I did I thought about what she said. When Dean graduated, I wanted him to be free to live life however he wanted.

I could only hope he wanted me and Finn to be a part of that life.

"FAVORITE SINGER OR band?" Dean asked. We lay tangled on the couch together, the television on low in the background. It was well past midnight, but I didn't want him to leave. My cheeks hurt from smiling so hard all night.

"Adele. You?"

"Anything old-school rock. Zeppelin, The Cure… Favorite color?"

"Blue." *Like your eyes*, I thought. "You?"

"Green. Like your eyes," he answered with a kiss on the tip of my nose.

My heart hammered in my chest. "Why do you ask me my favorites all the time?"

Dean grinned and then bent to kiss my lips. "I've never wanted to get to know a girl. I want to know every part of you and every favorite you have. Everything that makes you happy so that I can be the person who never lets you down and always brings you your favorites."

Oh my.

"Well, I want to know your favorites too. Let me think…" I tapped my finger on my chin. "Where's your favorite place for me to kiss you?" As soon as the question escaped from my mouth, the meaning hit my brain. Dean had a wicked gleam in his eyes, and I hid my face in his chest. "Oh, Lord. Did I just ask that?"

His chuckle rumbled beneath me. "You did. And I love your dirty little mind, Red. If I'm being honest, I can't answer that. Cause you haven't kissed me everywhere... yet."

Mortified. I was absolutely mortified. I had a choice. I could be shy and feel awkward, or I could own it.

Two seconds later I decided. I was owning it.

I raised my head and pressed a kiss on his chest. Then I lifted onto my elbows and shimmied a bit down his body.

"Let's rectify that, shall we?" I kissed further down his stomach, still on top of his shirt, and his body tensed.

"Grace, no. I was kidding. I didn't mean..."

I pressed up onto my hands and kissed his mouth. "I know you didn't. I want this. I want to feel you like this. To kiss you and lick you and..." His big body shuddered against me, and I hadn't even taken off his pants.

He leaned back against the arm of the couch and squeezed his eyes shut. "Red..."

Scooting down his body, I unbuttoned his jeans and pushed them down his legs. I stood and peeled them all the way off. Next I took his boxer briefs and pulled them down, throwing them onto the pile on the floor before I crawled back over him.

Dean's hands were balled into fists at his side, and his chest rose and fell in a rapid rhythm. I held him in my hand, and he groaned at just that contact. Leaning down, I ran my tongue over him, root to tip, and then sucked. Hard.

"Jesus *fucking* Christ!" Dean hissed, his eyes flying open. He bent one arm behind his head, and his abs contracted as he stilled the rest of his body.

I grinned, determined to own it. I dragged my tongue up and down the length of him, watching his eyes glued to mine. At the same time, I stroked him with my hand, and his eyes widened.

"Baby, oh God. That feels so… fucking… good."

I kept going but increased my speed and pressure, and his back arched. "You are so goddamn perfect, Red. Yes, shit. Fuck." I almost smiled, but that might take away from my owning it, so I refrained. I was so happy to hear his muttered curses, low groans, and raspy sounds. I wanted to bring Dean every pleasure possible. Just like he brought me.

"Move, baby. Move." He tried to shift, but I kept going. I wanted to take it all and give it all to him. To us. This was a huge step for me, but I was ready.

He came, eyes open and locked on mine, his lips pressed together to contain his roar. I kissed my way up his body, and he held me tightly to him. It took a few minutes for his breathing to slow, and once it did, I lifted my head.

"Favorite place to be kissed?" I asked with a wink.

He threw his head back and laughed. "I can't pick. Any place you put your lips on my body is my favorite." He rolled, placing his body on top of mine. "But I know my favorite place to kiss on yours. I think you do too."

I closed my eyes, already starting to pant in anticipation.

"Uh-uh. Eyes open, Red." He pulled my sweatpants and underwear off with one swift movement. "Watching your eyes as you took me in that perfect mouth was the hottest damn thing I've ever seen. I want your eyes on me the whole time I do the same."

I had no words. I nodded and bit my lip. My body shook as he brought his tongue to me, but I hung on and watched.

Gotta give him credit. He knew how to own it too.

"ARGH." I POUNDED my fist on the top of my ratty desk. The deep chuckle from behind caused me to smile despite my frustration. Dean and I were studying together. He was sprawled out on the couch while I typed a paper on economic solutions for third-world poverty.

Or at least I was trying to. My old laptop kept freezing up on me.

"What's up, Red?" Dean placed an arm on either side of my body and leaned over me to look at the computer screen.

His breath was warm against my cheek, and I shivered. The music didn't help either. Dean had used his portable speakers to play music from his iPhone while we worked. He had to be playing his sexy-time playlist to try to distract me. The soft melodic tunes were filling my brain and body with very uneconomic thoughts.

"Old Betty keeps freezing up on me," I whined.

"Old Betty?" He dragged his nose up the side of my neck, inhaling my scent.

"My laptop. Finn named her Betty. He went through a phase last year where he named everything in the apartment. The fridge is Fred." My voice was breathy from Dean's proximity. What I needed was to finish this paper and then jump him.

Dean laughed low and rough, and I crossed my legs in response. "Fred's a good one. Makes sense. You smell damn good, Red." Dean pressed his lips under my ear. "Reboot, baby."

I nodded and rebooted. "I'm so frustrated. I just want to finish this paper and then relax with you. Now I have to wait for it to restart." I stuck my lip out in a pout and crossed my arms over my chest.

"I'll distract you."

I opened my mouth to argue, but he shook his head.

"You'll stay right here. Don't have to move a muscle. As soon as the computer is up and running, I'll go finish studying, and you finish the paper." He moved my ponytail to the side and slid my shirt off my shoulder, exposing my thin bra strap and bare skin. "Give me five minutes, Red." He placed his mouth, lips parted, on my shoulder. He dragged his lips across the top of my shoulder, the tip of his tongue teasing me with light licks.

I closed my eyes and smiled, allowing him to take me away. Sexy music filled my ears, and my heart beat faster in my chest. Dean's mouth moved down the back of my shoulder and then up as he moved my bra strap down my arm, giving him full access to my shoulder and neck.

The pressure of his kisses and his tongue increased as he worked his way back up my neck and to my ear. My mouth opened in a silent gasp. He continued this path over and over again, adding in light bites and long drags of his tongue to my overheated and sensitive skin.

Top of shoulder, to the back of the shoulder, to neck, up to the ear.

Lips, teeth, tongue.

Over and over and over again.

I licked my lips as my core clenched and spasmed. The warmth, the softness, the intimacy of this moment was overwhelming.

He moved faster and pressed his mouth harder. He bit my earlobe, and my head fell back on his chest. I was panting now, mouth open, eyes still closed, feeling everything. He brought his hand to my breast, kneading it over the top of my shirt, and I whimpered.

All I heard was music. All I felt was Dean. All I needed was… more.

He was using both hands now, rubbing my breasts, pinching my hard nipples as he continued his assault of pleasure on my neck and ear, this time moving to the other side. My body lifted, still seated, but moving with him, pressing against him, not allowing him to break contact for even one second. He fisted my ponytail, using that leverage to move me from side to side, keeping me unable to predict where his mouth would be next.

When his mouth centered on the back of my neck, it tickled

my sensitive skin. I giggled and turned, my lips needing his. He kissed me back, not releasing his grip on my hair, but using it to guide us. We were frenzied, lips crashing and tongues dueling for control that I knew I never had and never would have around him.

He slowed our kiss, his tongue licking against mine ever so slightly as I came down from my high. I cupped the side of his face and kissed his lips, unable to hold back my grin.

My computer dinged, and he pulled back. "All set," he said as he wiggled the mouse and saw that the screen was unfrozen.

He kissed the top of my head and moved back to the couch as promised.

Dear Lord, he is good.

We were silent for a minute, and I wondered if he was really able to study after all that.

"What's the oven, Red?" Dean's voice was gruff. He was struggling too.

"Barney. Microwave's Wilma. There was a Flintstones phase too." I bit my lip and held back my laughter.

Turning behind me, Dean had his book open on his lap and head down. I stared at him, this sexy, beautiful, funny, man and I knew.

I could love this man.

Dean looked up and smirked, eyes flashing with heat. "Finish the damn paper, Red."

Giggling, I did just that. But I also finished my paper knowing that there was no *could.*

I was in love with this man.

chapter
Fifteen

Dean

EARLY MORNING WORKOUTS sucked. Luckily the day before a football game, Coach took it easy on us. Especially when
it was the day before the championship game and we were still
undefeated. I slipped on my hoodie and grabbed a Gatorade on
my way out the door.

I picked a song off my workout playlist to get me revved
up. Running on little sleep had become the norm. I hadn't spent
the night at Grace's, but I'd roll home in the early morning
hours.

Every minute of missed sleep was worth it, but I also needed to remain focused. As much as I wanted to be with Grace, I
had to win this game. We'd secure ourselves a good bowl game,
and my name would hopefully be on more lists for draft picks.

I dug out my earbuds, and my phone rang. My stomach
tightened when I saw Grace's name. We usually texted one another when we were awake for the day, but we were both too
busy to talk during the morning craziness.

I answered on the second ring. "Hey, Red. You okay?"

Grace sniffled into the phone, and my stomach sank. "No. Finn's sick. He has a fever, and he threw up this morning."

"Damn. I'm sorry, baby. What can I do? Want me to bring over some ginger ale?" My mind raced. What did my mom give us when we had the flu? Crackers or some shit? Popsicles. Hell yes! I should totally buy some Popsicles.

"I don't know what to do, Dean. I have a major exam first thing this morning. I can't bring him to daycare sick. I called Sylvie, and this bug must be going around. Everyone else called out of work. She has to wait all the tables by herself." Grace sounded more panicked than I had ever heard her. I had to fix this.

I didn't think twice before the words were out of my mouth. "I'll be there in ten. I'm running into the convenience store for some supplies. Get ready for your test."

"No. No, Dean. Don't you have practice? And your classes?"

"I only have exam reviews. I'm good. Let me help you. And after class, go to work. I'll call you if Finn gets worse. Sylvie can't work that place all by herself."

"Dean." Grace's voice cracked.

"Red, you let me in, right?" Grace sniffled, and I pictured her nodding and wiping her eyes. "I'm in. I'm here. I want to do this."

We ended the call as I walked into the food mart and grabbed a basket. There was no question in my mind that I would help them. Finn was important to me, and I would do anything in my power to make Grace's life easier. It almost didn't feel like I had a choice. They were my people, and they needed me. And so I would be there for them. Moving faster, I threw soda, Popsicles, soup, and crackers in my basket and hurried to the counter to pay. I jogged out of the store and toward Grace's apartment building.

I raised my fist to knock on her door, but it swung open. Grace threw herself into my arms.

"I've never had anyone offer to help me with him before. Not like this when he's sick. Not when you have to miss things in your life." Grace paused. "Thank you," she whispered into my neck.

I rubbed her back until she was ready to let go. "Take me to him?"

She nodded, and we walked into Finn's room. He was tossing and turning in his sleep. "He just took some Tylenol. I'm hoping he can keep it down. If he throws it up, wait a few hours before you give him more. If he keeps it down, he can have another two tablets in four hours." She handed me the medicine. "Text me with any questions. The thermometer is in the kitchen."

"We'll be fine. Go rock your exam." I settled on the floor next to Finn's bed and switched my phone to silent. All I needed was a text from Landon's dumb butt waking the kid up. Not on my watch.

Grace stood in front of me, her eyes darting between Finn and me. She looked down at her watch, and her eyes widened. "I have to go right now if I'm going to make it."

"Go. Run." I pointed toward the door, and she took off in a sprint.

I settled back and took in the little dude's space. The walls were plain white, probably because Grace wasn't allowed to paint university property. Instead, there were posters hung all over of Finn's favorite superheroes. A small bookshelf was filled with picture books, and there were lots of trucks, trains, and fire engines scattered around.

I pulled the blue blanket at Finn's feet up to his chin and pressed the palm of my hand on his forehead. He was warm but not burning hot. Finn moaned and moved to his side, facing me. His eyes opened, and when he saw my face, his lips curved upward in a smile.

"Dean?" His voice was raspy and weak.

I stood up and sat on the edge of his bed. "Your mom had to take a really important test today, and then she has to help Miss Sylvie out at the diner. Is it okay if I hang with you?"

Finn nodded, and his eyes drifted shut. "Did Superman have a daddy?"

My chest tightened. I swallowed before I answered him. "I think so, Just Finn."

He kept his eyes closed, but he smiled. "I think so too. I think Superman's daddy would be just like you."

Jesus. This kid was too damn sweet. My stupid ass eyes felt wet at the corners as I watched Finn fall back asleep. I belonged here. Grace and Finn made me feel like this was exactly where I was meant to be.

I sat on his bed and tried to process my thoughts. Grace didn't have anyone to turn to but me. I was fucking thrilled to be that person for her and Finn, but who would be there for her when I left next month? That thought made my stomach twist. We still hadn't talked about my leaving. I think we were both scared to talk about the next step and disturb the happiness we had found right now. But I believed with every part of me that Grace and I could make this work. I hoped to God she believe that too.

Once I knew Finn was sound asleep, I moved into the living room and turned on the sports channel. I pulled out my phone. *Fuck.* It was blowing up.

Jon: *Where are you?*

Jon: *The whole team is here for the meeting. Are you at Grace's? Text me some excuse, and I'll cover for you.*

Shit. Shit. Shit.

Jon: *You missed the meeting. We're starting warm-ups. Get your ass over here.*

Jon: *Coach is losing his mind, dude. You better be dead.*

Christ almighty. I was in serious trouble.

Coach K: *Dean, are you ill? Call the office immediately.*

My stomach rolled. Could I have already caught the flu from Finn? I called Coach and dragged my hand down my face. What was I going to say?

"Dean?" Coach answered right away. "Are you okay, son?"

I brought my fist to my forehead and knocked. *Think, ass-hole, think.* "Sir, I'm sorry. I had an emergency this morning."

Coach paused, most likely waiting for me to continue. "I'll ask you again, are you okay?"

"I'm fine, sir. My friend is, uh, sick and needed me. I'll come to the gym as soon as I can. It might be late this afternoon though."

Silence filled the line.

More silence.

Coach still didn't speak, and I was officially scared. Back when I was Finn's age, this would be where I'd be crapping in my pants.

"Goldsmith, you will be in my office today at four o'clock. If you're one minute late, you'll be benched tomorrow." My stomach landed on the floor. If Coach benched me, questions would be raised. Questions that could hurt my chances in the draft. That couldn't happen. "Do you hear me?"

I cleared my throat and willed my panic to settle. "Yes, sir."

"Be prepared to tell me the goddamn truth." Coach bit out his words. He was furious. The sound of the dial tone filled my ear.

I stared at the phone and then threw it on the table. I would not fuck this up. Not when I was this close.

I waited until I knew Grace's exam was over and then texted her.

Me: *I have a meeting at four. Can you be home by three thirty?*

None of this was Grace's fault. I wasn't mad at her in the least. But me? I was a stupid motherfucker. Just like I had promised myself I would never do, I was risking my future because I fell for a girl.

No, not just fell. I was in love with this girl.

I felt like I'd been hit by a truck. With a clarity I hadn't felt since I was a child and decided I wanted to play football as an adult, I knew exactly what I wanted. Grace and Finn were my priority. For the first time in my life, football hadn't come first.

Oh fuck. I slapped the palm of my hand against my head.

I was just like… Landon Washington.

chapter
Sixteen

Grace

I RACED INTO the diner at noon. I waved to Sylvie and then ran to the back room to get ready.

"Slow down, girl. I've got it under control." Sylvie popped her head in and frowned at me. "I hate it when you run here."

"You're..." I gasped for air. "All by yourself," I wheezed.

"No, I'm not." Sylvie turned me around so she could tie my apron strings. "Alejandro is cooking in the kitchen. I'm not alone. Besides, we're slow. I think half this town is sick."

I grabbed my pad and pencil and followed her into the restaurant. She pointed to a booth, and I made my way over, glancing at the day's specials on my way. "What can I get for you?" I looked down and saw Jon.

"Hi, Jon. How are you?" My smile was wide and friendly, but it slipped off my face when Jon's eyes narrowed.

"Do you have any idea where Dean is today?" Jon's mouth twisted, and his hands were clasped together on top of the table.

My head spun. I wouldn't lie, but I also wasn't sure what

Dean would want me to say. "Um, yes. He's at my apartment."

Jon's eyes bulged, and then he looked to his side. "Why in the hell is he there?" His jaw clenched, and he turned his head back to look at me.

I swallowed back the rock in my throat. "My son is sick." My words were a whisper. I felt so guilty even uttering them aloud. I should be home with him, not Dean.

"Dean's taking care of your son?" Jon asked himself the question. He groaned, and his head dropped down. "I knew this would happen. Shit."

"What? What happened?" I heard the fear in my voice. Jon motioned for me to sit across from him. I sat down, wringing my hands together under the table.

"Grace, he missed practice and the team meeting today. Friday." Jon stared at me, waiting for recognition to kick in. "The day before the championship game."

My mouth formed an "O," but I didn't speak. "If Coach didn't need him so badly to win, he'd bench him. That would affect his draft number."

I felt the color drain from my face. I pressed my fingertips to my lips.

"I've known Dean since we were six years old. All he's ever wanted was to play ball. He's worked every year for this exact moment. To end college with a winning season and make it into the draft. To get placed as a quarterback on an NFL team. And he's this close." Jon held his finger and thumb up, a smidgeon of space between the two. "He's almost there, and now he's confused."

He paused and took a drink of his water. "Has Dean talked to you about what will happen when he moves home at the end of the month?"

I traced circles on the tabletop with my fingertips. "No."

Jon frowned. "Has he made any kind of commitment to you? Any promise to only be with you when he leaves?"

I didn't look up. I didn't want to see the pity in his eyes. "We haven't talked at all about what will happen with us after he graduates."

Jon placed his hand over mine, and I stilled. "Has he said he loves you?"

I waited a beat before I looked up. The lump in my throat was so big it ached when I swallowed. "No." I mouthed.

Jon leaned forward. "I've only told a few people in my life this, but I'm going to tell you. I grew up without a dad. My mom was always a single mom. Like you, she was beautiful. Still is." He smiled. "So she dated. A lot. Over the years guys were always around. They never stayed. Never committed. Never loved her, I guess." Jon took another drink of his water, and tears filled my eyes. "As an adult I can say that was their loss, but as a kid… Grace, I thought it was me. I thought if they left it was because I wasn't good enough. Because they didn't love me."

He looked away, his own eyes shiny. I reached out and held his hand.

"Since the moment I saw that Dean had set his sights on you, I've been worried. Football has always come first for him, and you have a kid. I've been that kid. I can't sit back and watch you fall in love with him and know your son is falling in love with him too, only to have him leave. And he will, Grace. He will put football first. Where does that leave your son?" he paused. "I know where it left me. Fucked up."

I had these thoughts, these fears. I just hoped and prayed that we'd find a way to make it work. "Jon, I hear you. I swear to God I do, but you're wrong about Dean." My voice cracked, and I blew out a breath. "I think he really likes having Finn in his life. Maybe he can have both—us and football. "

Jon looked thoughtful as he rubbed his chin. "He told me he wished you didn't have a kid. That everything would be so much easier without your son in the picture." Jon stopped speaking and stared at me. "One of my mom's boyfriends said that about me when he dumped her. I'll never forget it." I could tell this was really hurting him to talk about. On a hard swallow that worked his throat, Jon continued. "Dean's my best friend, but he's not ready to be a daddy, Grace. If he was, he wouldn't have said that to me."

Rage and sadness and utter devastation filled me. *He wished I didn't have Finn?* My throat was so dry I grabbed Jon's glass of water and gulped it down. "Thank you for talking to me and for trusting me with your past. I'm so sorry about the way you grew up. You have my word that I won't let Finn feel the way you did." Time to get control of my life back. I stood up and pulled out my pad. "Can I get you anything to eat?"

Jon's eyebrows pulled together. "I don't want food, Grace. I only came here to talk to you."

I nodded and placed the pad in my apron pocket. "And I heard you loud and clear. I'll handle it." Jon still looked unsure. I placed both hands on the table and leaned close to Jon. "I love Dean." He closed his eyes, but I kept going. "But my son comes first. Always and every time. There's no way I'd ever be with someone who wished I didn't have Finn in my life or who has more important priorities." Jon's delivery was rough, but he was right. If Dean didn't want my son in my life, it was my job to end our relationship. I was Finn's protector, and if I didn't protect him, Dean would end up hurting him.

Just like I was hurting now.

Jon opened his eyes and nodded. I blinked back my tears and headed to Sylvie. "I'm so sorry. I have to go. Will you be okay?"

Sylvie nodded and patted my hand. "Of course. Go be with your boys."

Boy. I only had one boy in my life. Just like it had always been.

I EASED OPEN the door to my apartment, unsure if I'd find Finn asleep. Instead, Dean and Finn were curled up on the couch both sucking on green Popsicles. Cartoons blared from the television, and they had a blanket spread around their legs.

I wanted to smile, but instead, tears filled my eyes. I wouldn't see this again, and that already caused an ache to fill my heart. More powerful than the ache, though, was the anger.

"Hiya, Mommy! We're watching a movie on Clark Kent." Finn beamed. "And I feel better. No more throw up."

"That's great, buddy." I walked over and kissed his forehead.

Dean pulled the Popsicle from his lips with a long slurp. "I learned the television's name today. Clark Kent." He grinned proudly. "Fever's gone too, Mama."

I avoided Dean's eyes. "Good. Thank you." I stood up and walked to the front door. "You should go. I know you said you had a meeting at four, but Sylvie let me go early."

Dean walked into the kitchen and tossed his Popsicle in the trash. He walked over and cupped my face. "You sure? She was okay without you?"

I pulled out of his grasp. "Of course." My stomach flipped, and my head pounded.

"Grace? What's wrong?" Dean reached for me, and I stepped backward. His face fell, and my heart plummeted to the floor.

I crossed my arms over my chest. I summoned all the anger I had inside and pushed away the sorrow. "I saw Jon at the diner. He told me you missed your team meeting and practice."

Dean inhaled sharply and rubbed the back of his neck. "He should have kept his damn mouth shut."

My arms flung open and out to my sides. "Why did you do

that? You could be benched tomorrow. You could hurt your chances in the draft. Why did you do something so stupid?"

"Stupid?" Dean bit out the word. His eyes flashed, and he stepped closer to me. "You think watching your son while he's sick is stupid?"

"No." I lowered my voice to a whisper. "I'm the one that's stupid. I should have contacted my professor and told her the situation. I should have never put you in that position." I stepped closer to him. "And you shouldn't have offered to help, Dean." I rubbed my temples, the pounding in my head intensifying. "I've been thinking." I looked up, and his face was void of any emotion. Only the clenching and unclenching of his jaw let me know that he was anticipating my words. "We've gotten too close, too fast." I swallowed and then blew out a breath. "I think we need to end this now."

Dean stared at me. "What? Why?"

"You're leaving. I can't put Finn through that. It would be too hard on him. It's better to do this sooner rather than later." I left it at that. If I told Dean I knew what he had said to Jon, if he realized I had found out what he really thought about Finn, he'd deny it. I didn't want to tarnish this further with lies. I'd rather end things peacefully than repeat Jon's words. They hurt too much.

Dean's eyes widened. "No. Grace, c'mon. We can make this work. People have long-distance relationships all the time."

"Kid's don't." I held my hands out in front of me. "Think about Finn. We have to do what's best for him."

Dean stepped closer to me and held my hand in his. "I think you and I together are pretty damn good for him."

I yanked my hand away. "You're not listening to me. We won't be together. You'll be gone. My son needs a consistent man in his life. He needs a man with a regular job and stability. Someone who can really be there for him. None of those things go with the spotlight of the NFL. It isn't fair to string us along like this when you're just going to leave at the end of the semester. You're being selfish and only thinking about yourself."

Dean closed his eyes. "Wow." When he opened them they were flat and seemed lifeless. "I didn't know that's what you thought about me. You may not believe this, but I've thought about you and Finn every day since I met you. I'm sorry you can't see that." I watched him walk into the family room, whisper something in Finn's ear, and walk out the front door. I sank to the floor, the tears I held back rolling down my cheeks.

I used to think Dean was truly happy we were in his life. That was until I found out he wished Finn wasn't in *my* life. I wiped my tears away. I did the right thing. My son would always come first. Dean didn't want to be saddled with the responsibility of a girlfriend with a child. He needed to focus on his future. And my only focus was on Finn's. That was all that mattered.

I loved those two boys. I loved them enough to put their needs first.

Even if they didn't know it.

chapter
Seventeen

Dean

THE HOOD OF my sweatshirt covered my head. I couldn't see anyone I knew right now. I had to get myself under control. I walked at a fast clip to the athletic center. I'd be early to meet Coach, but I had nowhere else to go.

What I wanted was a fight. I wanted to punch something, or better yet, someone. I had tried so fucking hard. I had tried to be a good man. Like Landon had. But she didn't want me. Grace didn't trust me.

She wanted someone else for Finn. Someone better than me.

I punched at my chest. *Man up, Goldsmith.* You are not a pussy. This is one girl. One chick. That's all.

I was a bad liar even when I was lying to myself.

Other than a fight, getting drunk off my ass was another enticing option. Couldn't happen though. The biggest game of my college career was tomorrow. I opened the door to the football offices and walked down the empty hallway. My teammates were resting and fueling up for tomorrow. They were home centering themselves while I felt like a cyclone of anger and emotion. This was so fucking bad.

I knocked on Coach's door and waited.

"Come in," Coach K called.

I opened the door and walked to his desk. Papers were spread all around, and a video of our opponents' game highlights was playing in the background. Coach looked up and frowned. "Sit down, son."

I sat in the chair and fixed my gaze on the television.

"Who is she?" Coach leaned back in his squeaky chair and folded his hands behind his head.

"Excuse me, sir?"

Coach raised his eyebrows and stared me down.

I bit back a grin. The crotchety old guy knew me pretty well. He knew all his players pretty well. "Her name's Grace."

Coach nodded. "And she's ill? You missed practice to help her?"

"No." I looked down at the floor for a second before I grew a pair and looked my coach in the eyes. "I missed practice to help her son, Finn. He was sick."

Coach's eyes widened. "She has a kid? Is she a student here?"

I sat back in my chair. "Coach, she's an amazing girl. She's a senior, and she's been attending IU while raising her son at the same time. She has no one. No family. She's all alone. She only called me for help because there was no one else to ask." I took off my baseball cap and tugged at my hair. "I wouldn't have missed practice or the meeting if there was any other choice. She had an exam, and Finn had a fever and was throwing up. He couldn't go to daycare."

Coach stared at me, then leaned his head back and looked up at the ceiling. "Are you in love with her, Dean? Or should I ask, with both of them?"

My stomach felt like it was full of boulders. I pictured

Grace and Finn at their apartment. I pictured kissing her and tickling him and Thanksgiving dinner together. I saw the way she loved him and the way he adored every hair on her head. I thought about being alone again and missing being a part of their lives.

"Yes, sir. I love them both. But my semester ends in two weeks. I'll move home and then hopefully leave for training. I'm not sure if I'm good for them right now."

Coach nodded and moved his clasped hands onto the top of his head. "I'm your football coach, son. But I've gotten to know you over these four years. You're an excellent quarterback, but you're also a good man. I've seen you take care of the young guys and show respect to the older ones, even when you were a stronger player. You're going to get invited to the scouting combine. You're going to get drafted. I've been around long enough. I know this." Coach stood up and walked over to me. He perched on the front of his desk. "You're young. Are you ready to be with just one girl? 'Cause, Dean, your life will change when you go pro. If you want a serious relationship with a girl who has a kid, you have to be one hundred percent sure. You'll be tempted. You have to think all of this through."

I swallowed and nodded. "Is it fair to ask her to stay here alone and finish school while I'm away for months? And then is it fair to ask her to move with me to whichever team picks me? I'm struggling with that. I mean, she just broke up with me, so I'm thinking it's not even an issue, but…"

Coach's mouth formed a flat line. He grunted and scratched the back of his head. "I got married during college." Coach smiled, and I bit my cheek to keep from laughing. Holy shit, he actually smiled. "Heidi and I met and fell in love when we were eighteen. I asked her to marry me at nineteen. Everybody thought she was with child, but she wasn't. She turned my proposal down three times. She told me I should wait and find someone better. She told me we were too young. She told me she wanted me to have fun and party before I settled down." Coach crossed his arms and looked at me, his ruddy cheeks a bit darker as he talked about Heidi.

"Thing is, son, I knew she was my girl. I loved her, and I wanted to be with her. We got married at twenty and lived in family housing at college. We were young, but we were in love. Nothing better than that." He cleared his throat. "My point is, if you love her and only her, then you need to decide what you want. If she and her son are what you want, don't hold back. You can have a career in the pros and a personal life. It's not an either or. You both can make this work."

Well, shit. This was not the conversation I expected to have with my coach. I stood up and extended my hand. "Thank you, sir. I'd love to meet Heidi, er, uh Mrs. Kirkpatrick one day."

Coach shook my hand, but his face fell. "She died from cancer ten years ago. That's what I'm saying, son. Don't waste a minute in this life. It's gone before you know it." Coach turned around and coughed.

Damn. "I'm sorry, sir. I'm real sorry."

Coach turned back to me and handed me an envelope. "Tickets to tomorrow's game have been sold out forever." I nodded. I'd gotten my parents tickets, but I couldn't get any for my siblings, and they were pissed. "Why don't you invite your Grace and her son? Talk to her afterward and tell her how you feel."

I took the envelope. Should I give him a hug? Was that appropriate? I stepped forward with my arms in front of me and Coach reared back.

"Get the hell out, Goldsmith. Get some dinner and then sleep. And so help me God, if you're late tomorrow morning..." He held a finger up in warning. Coach was back.

I laughed and walked backward. "No, sir. I'll be early. I'm going to drop these off now."

Coach looked down at his desk, studying his papers. As I

jogged down the hallway, my stomach twisted.

I wanted to tell Grace I loved her, but I wasn't sure she was ready for that. At the very least I wanted to tell her that I wanted her and Finn in my life no matter what. I could be the man that Finn needed. Coach was right. We could make this work.

I hoped to God she heard me. That she believed me. The next few weeks would change my life, and I knew exactly who I wanted to share it with. The little dude owned a superhero's costume complete with a cape. The girl owned my heart.

chapter
Eighteen

Grace

I KISSED FINN'S cheek and turned out his light. He was still fighting off the virus, so he'd fallen asleep early. I walked back into the kitchen and heard a knock on my door.

I checked the peephole and saw Dean. With his baseball cap pulled low on his head, his expression was unreadable.

As much I wanted to hide and pretend he wasn't there or that I wasn't home, I knew I had to face the music. I learned the truth about his feelings, but he didn't know that. I wouldn't throw Jon under the bus for telling me. He had known Dean his whole life, and he cared about him. As angry as I was at Dean, a part of me understood how he felt. My life hadn't been easy since Finn. Unlike him, though, I never wished it were different. Despite all of that, I still cared about Dean.

So much that it was killing me to have to say good-bye to him.

I opened the door and moved to the side. Dean's face softened as soon as he saw me.

"Hey," he said taking a deep breath. "Can we talk?"

I nodded, and Dean closed the door. We walked to the couch and sat facing each other. Dean handed me an envelope just like he had two months ago. "Please come to the game tomorrow. These are free tickets to the family section. My parents will be there. I want to introduce them to you and Finn. Don't give up on us. I want you in my life."

I placed the envelope on the coffee table and slid it over to him. "No, we can't do that. It isn't a good idea for us to come to the game or to meet your family." I twisted my fingers together as my heart slammed against my chest.

He blew out a breath. "Do you believe what you said? That I'm not a good enough man to be in Finn's life? You really want to break up with me?"

I licked my lips. "I don't *want* to break up, but it's for the best." Jon's words ran through my brain in a loop. "You're a good man, Dean, but you're not ready for a family. This is the time to end things before they get too complicated."

Dean released my hand and moved his baseball cap backward. I could fully see his face, and my words had gutted him. "I think we've already complicated things, Red. But I've never been happier than when I'm with this family." He pressed his lips together.

I placed my hands on his bent knee. "Dean, listen to me. You're being careless, and people are going to get hurt."

Dean flinched. "How am I being careless?"

"You're careless with your future. You missed practice and your meeting. That could have cost you your dream." I took a shaky breath. "I can't be the reason your dreams are destroyed. I already destroyed Josh's life and his dreams and look what happened. I won't destroy yours, and I don't want you to regret having us in your life. I live each day thinking about the people that regret having had me in their lives."

Dean narrowed his eyes. "You've destroyed nothing. Josh

was sick, baby. You didn't cause him to kill himself. And your parents and Josh's parents are cowards." He stood up, pacing in front of me. "You never asked me to skip my practice today. I knew full well what I was doing. And I sure as hell wasn't being careless." His voice was louder, raw with emotion and anger. "I've never cared about *anything* more than I care about you and Finn."

I shook my head back and forth. "You're being careless right now with Finn's heart and mine. You're leaving, and we've made no commitments to each other. What does that mean for my son?" My stomach turned upside down, and my chest tightened. I wasn't getting through to him. I couldn't seem to get enough air into my lungs at the thought of speaking the truth aloud. "I know how you feel about him. You wish I didn't have a child."

Dean's eyes formed slants, his lips pursed together, and his tanned skin flashed red. I could only imagine how red my skin was. His hands formed into fists, and he dragged in a breath. "What the hell are you saying?"

"You heard me. You wish I didn't have Finn. Admit it. Be honest, for God's sake." My chest heaved, and tears filled my eyes. I knew the truth. I heard it from his best friend. Why couldn't he admit it? How could he lie to my face?

"No! No, Grace. I don't wish that. Finn means the world to me. I adore him."

"You do not. Don't lie. We're just an easy way to pass time before you leave." My head spun. I felt drunk and out of control. I was sure I sounded unreasonable, but I had never meant my words more. I hated him for making me fall in love with him. He made my son love him too, and it hurt to know that all that time he wished he never existed.

Just like my parents. Just like Josh.

"You think I'm lying?" he roared, pulling on his hair.

"Why are you doing this to us?" I swallowed hard against

the lump in my throat. "We were better off before you came around and showed us what we were missing. God knows your life will be *easier* without Finn in it." The words burned liked lava coming from my mouth. His body jolted as he took them in.

"Mama? Why are you yelling? Why is Dean lying?" Finn's sleepy voice shocked me, and I jumped back.

"Finn, baby, go back to bed." I knelt down and kissed his forehead.

Finn's chin quivered. "No, tell me! Tell me, Mama. Dean's life is easier without me?" Finn's voice was high pitched with fear.

"No way, Just Finn. I like everything more with you around." Dean spoke in a low, calm voice as he walked over to us.

"No!" I shouted, and Finn jumped. "Don't do this to him. Don't act like you're still going to be here once the New Year comes. It's not fair. I want you to leave."

"I don't want Dean to go," Finn cried out, his eyes filling with tears.

I brushed a tear from his cheek. "We knew all along that he was leaving, baby. We talked about this. Dean's getting ready to graduate college. Then he's going to play football, and we will see him on television. But that's it."

"Grace," Dean interrupted. "I don't want to—"

"No!" I shouted, and Finn sobbed.

Finn pointed at Dean. "You cracked my heart." Turning, he looked me right in the eye. "And I hate you."

"Finn!" Dean called, but Finn ran to his room and slammed his door. "Red." Dean's voice was ragged. I looked up at his shiny eyes, and my own heart cracked open.

I couldn't look at him any longer. "Please just go."

He moved the envelope back in front of me. "Get some sleep, and then come tomorrow. We can work all this out later. It's the biggest game of my life. There is no one I want there more than you. Please, Red. I need you there. Both of you."

I didn't answer him. I stayed on my knees, my eyes rooted on the worn tan carpet until I heard the door click.

And then I crawled onto the couch and cried myself to sleep.

"ARE YOU SURE you can make it to your exam?" Amy's mom, Clare, asked. "You've been sick for a week. Dan told me he could get all of your exams rescheduled."

I bent over to tie my shoe, and my hands shook. "I'll be fine. You've stayed with me this whole time. I'll never be able to repay you and Amy for your kindness." I had no intention of calling in favors with Dan, Amy's dad. I had to join the land of the living again.

Clare rubbed my back, and tears pricked at my eyes. The past week had been hell. I didn't even remember texting Amy on Saturday morning. All I knew was that Amy and Clare arrived and told me I was burning up with a fever. They moved me into Finn's room to keep me quarantined and settled into the family room with inflatable mattresses. I spent the next days in a fog, throwing up and sleeping almost constantly. Clare and Amy had taken Finn to daycare each day, fed him, played with him, bathed him, and put him to bed. They even managed to convince Finn that they were having a giant sleepover in the family room. They rescued me, and I couldn't have managed without them.

"I'm happy we could help you, Grace. You scared us for a while. I still think we should have taken you to the hospital." She handed me a Gatorade, and I sipped.

When Clare had roused me from sleep on day four to announce we were going to the hospital, I had a total meltdown. I begged and pleaded until she gave in. The fact was I couldn't afford those bills and I couldn't be away from Finn. What if the hospital contacted child services? Clare and Amy weren't family. If someone tried to take Finn from me, I would die. Plain and simple. He was all I had to live for.

"I'm okay." I powered my phone on and slipped it into my pocket. "I'm not back to normal, but I'm good enough. Go home and back to your life. Thank you, Clare."

We hugged, and I walked her to her car. As I turned toward Ballantine Hall, I looked at my phone. Amy told me that Dean had called repeatedly on Saturday, so they turned off my phone. I wasn't able to speak with my virus, let alone deal with that emotional minefield. I saw twelve missed texts from Dean, but I couldn't read them right before my exam. I had to concentrate and pass this course. I couldn't afford to fail a class and delay my graduation.

I reached into the other pocket of my jeans and pulled out a note from Finn. Amy told me that Finn fell apart when I got so sick. He believed he gave me the virus and that I hated him because he told me he hated me. As soon as I could sit up, we spoke, and I tried to reassure him, but he was thrown. I opened the picture. We stood together—Dean, Finn, and me—at the park, holding hands. "I sorry, Mama" was scrawled in crayon along the bottom of the page.

I choked back a sob as I folded the paper and put it into my pocket.

"Grace?" A hand gripped my forearm before I started up the stairs. I knew that voice. I wasn't ready to hear that voice.

I looked to my left. "Hi, Dean." My throat was dry, and my voice was weak.

Dean's eyebrows pulled together. "Are you okay?"

I nodded and ran a hand through my hair. Even my hair seemed affected by this virus. The shiny red was dulled and thin. "Yes, just caught a cold."

Dean looked me up and down. "Just a cold? You've lost a

ton of weight."

I pulled away from him. "No, I haven't." Total lie. I'd lost over ten pounds. I looked like I was only made of skin and bones. I would see Sylvie for the first time today at work, and I was pretty sure she would immediately force-feed me a bacon cheeseburger.

"I've called. And texted." Dean looked away and then back at me. "You never came to the game, Red. Please talk to me."

I looked down at my watch. "I have an exam. I have to go." I started up the stairs and then turned around. *Be brave, Grace. Do what is best for Finn and Dean and cut all ties.* "Please make this easier on all of us and just let me go." I watched his face fall, and then he turned around, walking out of my life.

He thought I'd let him go. The problem was, once I let him in and allowed myself to love him, I would never be able to let Dean Goldsmith go. Even though in the end, I always knew he would.

But that was for me to deal with. Right now I had a test to pass.

chapter
Nineteen

Dean

THE FANCY-ASS PEN felt heavy in my hand. "Sign here." Andrew pointed to another line, and I scrawled my name across the bottom. My now-official agent held out his hand, and we shook. "I'm looking forward to making you a very rich man, Dean."

I smiled. That was all I had right now. Andrew stood in the kitchen I grew up in and talked to my parents. Mom and Dad had liked him, and that was good enough for me. After winning the championship game, and as soon as my eligibility was announced from IU, agents had been contacting me left and right. I liked that Andrew had been the first one to approach me.

Andrew clasped my shoulder. "Have a great Christmas. I'll see you in Florida." IU was playing at the Citrus Bowl in Orlando on New Year's Day, and my new agent wouldn't miss it. He waved and made his way out the door. He had wanted that contract signed pretty damn bad to drive out here on Christmas Eve.

Business first, I guess. Football had always come first to me too.

Until now.

Focus, Goldsmith. Focus on football.

Andrew's firm had secured me a spot in a training facility in Arizona for right after the senior bowl game at the end of the month. This game was for the best senior collegiate players in the country, who were also the top NFL draft prospects. After that I'd be training all day for the NFL combine at the end of February. I would find out in a few days if I was invited to the combine, but everyone around me was confident. Except for me. At a time in my life when I should be overflowing with self-assurance, I was weak. What I believed and what I knew weren't true. Grace didn't want me in her life. She believed my life was easier without them. The gaping hole in my chest kept me off-balance.

"Mom Goldsmith!" Landon's voice boomed through the kitchen. He jogged to my mom and lifted her off her feet in a giant hug.

My dad rounded the table. "Hello, Emma." My father kissed her cheek and Emma grinned.

"Merry Christmas, Mr. and Mrs. Goldsmith." Emma unwrapped her scarf and took off her gloves. "It's so cold! I'm happy to see you all, but part of me wishes we had stayed in California this year."

I walked over and hugged Emma. As I passed by Landon, I smacked him on the back of the head. "Your phone dead, numbnut? When did you get into town?"

Landon rubbed his head. "Ow. We just got in this morning. We spent some time with Evie and Garrett and then came straight here. Chill."

That made me grin. I should've known. Evie was Emma's sister, and Garrett was her live-in boyfriend. Both had different special needs. They were cool people, and I'd learned a lot from them, just like I had from Amy.

Dad slapped Landon on the back. "How are you, son? Graduating soon?" He motioned to the chairs, and we all sat around my parents' table. Mom placed a platter of sugar cookies in the middle.

"Sweet! Thanks, Mom G." Landon shoved an entire cookie in his mouth and chewed. Emma's nose wrinkled as she watched him.

"Why are you still with that animal, Emma?" I made a gagging noise in the back of my throat, and she laughed, shrugging her shoulders. Landon extended his hand around the back of both my parents and shot me his middle finger.

"I still have another year and a half, Mr. G. I'm graduating with an undergraduate degree and a masters in special education. I'll go right into the classroom when I'm finished." Landon answered my father before he grabbed another cookie.

"Landon is fantastic with special needs kids, Mr. Goldsmith. We help run a camp every summer, and the kids adore him. He'll be the best teacher." She leaned over and kissed Landon's cheek.

"Thanks, baby." Landon slung his arm over Emma's shoulder, pulling her in closer to him.

My stomach twisted. I was *fucking* jealous. In the past anytime I'd ever witnessed Landon falling all over Emma, I felt nothing. That's not true. I pitied him. I wished for him the life that I had. Filled with nothing but football and females. And now I was jealous. I wanted Grace next to me and Finn on my lap, giving himself a belly ache from my mom's cookies and hot chocolate.

But according to Grace, they were better off without me. *Bullshit.*

"Where's the rest of the clan? All your brothers and sisters? The little Deans and Deanettes?" Landon asked, arching his neck to look around the kitchen.

My mother pulled out a chair and joined us at the table.

"Last-minute Christmas shopping. Devin drove them in the van."

"Darn. The highlight of my visit home is when the five of them gang up on Dean." Landon chuckled, and my Dad nodded.

Seems my siblings weren't the only ones who ganged up on me.

"Mr. and Mrs. Goldsmith? And Dean? I asked Amy to come over here too. Is that all right? We're going to drive her home later and visit with her parents." Emma sipped from the mug of hot chocolate my mom handed her.

"Of course! Any of your friends are welcome here," my dad said.

"Glad to hear that. Merry Christmas everybody!" Jon called out as he walked into the kitchen. Ricky followed behind him.

"Merry, merry," Ricky mumbled. He was the least jolly motherfucker I had ever seen. I needed to find out what was going on with that guy. Ever since we left for college and he stayed behind, he'd changed. And not for the better.

Mom passed around more steaming mugs of hot chocolate, kissing each of my friends on the cheek as she delivered their drink.

Landon piled his mug high with a handful of marshmallows. He still drank his hot chocolate like a six-year-old. At least some things never changed. "Congrats on graduating early, man. We can't wait to catch the bowl on television. Are you bringing your girl with you to Florida?" Landon grinned, and I balled my hands into fists under the table. Not his fault. He didn't know what went down. Fact was, it still hurt like a motherfucker to hear someone refer to Grace as my girl.

My parents exchanged a look before turning to me. "Your girl? Is this the one we waited to meet at the football game?" My mom crossed her arms over her chest. She was furious when Grace was a no-show. No matter how old or ugly I got, I was her baby boy, and she wasn't okay with anyone hurting me.

Emma's face fell. "She didn't come to your game? Was

something wrong with her son?"

My dad stood up. "She has a kid?" His face reddened, and I looked up at the ceiling and blew out a breath. *Thanks so much for coming over, Landon and Emma.*

"Dad, please sit down." I scooted my chair back from the table. Emma mouthed an apology to me as Landon rubbed her back. Jon stared at the table, and Ricky looked as confused as I felt.

"Tell us what happened, man," Landon urged.

I ran my hands through my hair. They all loved me, or at least tolerated me as was the case with Emma. "Mom, Dad, I met a girl named Grace a few months ago. She has a four-year-old son who she's raised alone while going to college full time."

"Whoa." My dad's eyes widened, and he rubbed his chin.

Mom sat forward and clasped her hands in front of her on the table. "Are her parents present in their lives?"

I shook my head. "They wanted her to get an abortion." Mom gasped, and Emma slapped her hand across her mouth. "When she refused, they threw her out. Disowned her. Her pregnancy, the birth of her son, every holiday... It's just the two of them." My throat was rough as I swallowed. The sour feeling in my stomach grew as it did whenever I thought about Grace's life.

"And what happened to the kid's dad?" Landon's voice was gruff. Landon's dad disowned him when he lost his scholarship to IU. He knew the feeling of bitter disappointment both from and in a parent. "Where has he been?"

I looked down to the floor. "He died by suicide." Landon's curse and my mom's cry was all I heard. When I surveyed the table, Dad had his eyes closed. My friends looked at each other with wide eyes. "He suffered from depression, and when Grace told him she was pregnant during their senior year of high school, he snapped. He knew he'd let his parents down, and his life was changed. He decided to end it." My voice cracked, and I got up and walked to the sink. I grabbed a glass from the cabinet and filled it with water, drinking a large gulp.

Mom walked behind me and placed a hand on my back. "Why didn't she come to the game, Dean? It sure sounds like she needs someone like you in her life. Someone who cares for her."

I turned to face the group. "I thought she did. I love her. God, I love both of them so much. I was ready to commit to her. To tell her she was all I wanted."

"What happened?" Emma asked.

"Finn got sick, and I skipped practice to stay home with him. When she came home that day from work, something had changed. I don't know what the hell happened. She had a bunch of reasons why we shouldn't be together anymore." I slammed the glass of water down on the counter. "She broke up with me." I dragged my hands through my hair. "She was convinced I wished she didn't have a son. I don't know where she got that idea." My stomach hurt at the recollection.

"Shit, Dean." Jon stood up and walked over to me. He rubbed the back of his shaved head. "You mean that? You're in love with Grace?"

I threw my arms out to the side. "Yes! And I don't understand what the fuck happened."

Jon looked away. "I do. This is all my fault."

My blood began to boil. This was bad. I was going to have to hurt my best friend. "What do you mean?" I leaned in so close to Jon that our noses touched. Landon's chair scraped against the floor as he pushed it back and jumped between us. Ricky followed and moved to the other side of Jon.

"Settle down, boys." My dad's voice boomed across the room. "There are ladies present. Jon, tell Dean what you know. Help him make some sense of this mess."

Jon nodded, and Landon pushed me back another step. "I went to Maria's Diner looking for Grace when you didn't show up for practice." He swallowed hard.

"I know that. Grace told me that you were the one that told her I missed practice and the meeting. She didn't say that you said more," I growled.

Jon took a deep breath. "I told her that you've worked your whole life to get right where you are now. To go pro. To play ball for a living. And that by skipping the meeting and practice, you'd jeopardized that."

I reached out and fisted his shirt. "What else did you say, you stupid ass?"

"I told her about me. The way I grew up."

I released Jon's shirt and took a step back. You could have heard a pin drop, the room was so silent. Jon rarely talked about his family, but when he did, it wasn't good.

"I knew you were over there playing house, and it brought me right back to the guys who acted like I mattered to them but then moved on. Away. I thought... that would happen to her kid. I didn't think you'd want a serious relationship when you were heading to the pros. I thought you'd get tired of them, and the kid would end up hurt."

His voice dropped low, but I heard every goddamn word that came next. "And I told her what you said on the bus that one time."

The bus? My mind raced. "What was that?"

Jon looked at Landon over my shoulder, and Landon's grip on me tightened. *Fuck.* "I told her you wished she didn't have a kid."

My mom and Emma both yelled my name in a tone that hinted Jon wasn't the only one getting hit tonight.

I raised my fist, and Jon yelled out, "I'm sorry, man. You pissed me off when you said that."

Landon held my arms back as I clamored to get at Jon's face. "I never said that you jackass!"

"You did. After the Ohio game. Remember? You said it would be easier to be with her without a kid. Some guy said the same thing to my mom. And it sucks, okay?"

Jesus Christ. Jon would pay for this shit. "You bag of dicks. This is not the same thing that happened to you. Yes of course kids make things harder for anyone at any stage of their relationship. Remember the next thing I said? That I didn't mind things being complicated? That I dug both of them so much? That I wanted them to be a part of my world and vice versa? You tell her any of that, asshole?"

Jon paled. "I fucked up. I thought you felt sorry for her and her kid. I didn't know you freaking loved her. I mean, she said she loved you, but I just thought…"

The sound of rushing air filled my ears. My head spun, and I dropped my fist, stumbling backward.

"Calm down, fucker. Calm down and listen." Landon spoke in my ear, and I dragged in a breath.

"She said she loves me?" My voice was raw, and my throat burned.

"She got pissed, man. She got right in my face and told me she loved you but that she could never be with anyone who didn't want her son in their life." Jon looked right into my eyes. "She looked real sad, but now that I hear her whole story… She's had it so rough. Damn, man. I'm sorry."

I stared at him. I hated that Jon had a bad childhood, and I sort of got that he was trying to protect Finn from that, but he went too far. He hurt my Grace, and he would be getting punched for it. Right in the face. I knew it, and he knew it. But not in my mom's kitchen.

"Dean, you both love each other. Have you tried to talk to her since she ended it? This sounds like one huge misunderstanding." My mom wiped her eyes with a tissue.

I scrubbed my hands over my face. "Yeah, I went to her and begged her to reconsider breaking up with me." Landon snickered, relishing my new president-level status in the land of pussy, but I ignored him. He had every right to mock me. I may be acting even worse than he did when he lost Emma. "I gave her tickets to the game the next day and told her I wanted her to meet my parents, but she never showed up. I kept calling even after the game. She never returned my messages or texts."

"She was sick. Very, very sick." Amy stood in the doorway, frowning.

Everyone froze. I walked over to her slowly. "How do you know that, Amy?"

Amy's smile was small. "She does love you. She kept saying it all through the fever."

My stomach plummeted to the ground. I thought I might puke. I didn't feel sick before the championship game, but this whole day was bringing me to my knees.

Emma walked over to Amy and hugged her. "When did Grace get a fever, Amy?"

Amy looked at Emma and then at me. "Sometime early that Saturday. She texted me that she was sick, and my mom and I went to her house. She was burning up. I took care of Finn." She beamed with pride. "For seven whole days."

My mom drew in a sharp breath. "A week! Did Grace go to the hospital, sweetie? Is she okay?"

Amy nodded. "My mom took care of her the whole time. After a few days we tried to take her to the hospital. She was so hot and kept throwing up. She could not talk. Finn was scared. But she would not go."

Emma's hand was pressed against her chest. "Why not?"

"She did not have money to pay the bills. And she worried that someone would try and take Finn from her," Amy said with a frown.

I slumped onto the floor, my head between my knees.

"Fuck me," Jon muttered.

A tear ran down my face, and I didn't give a shit that my boys saw it. She loved me. Red loved me. She had been sick and scared, and I wasn't there for her. Like everyone else in her life.

"Dean?" Amy crouched down next to me on the floor. "Do you love her? Or are you trying to save her? Because she does not need you to save her. She already loves a superhero."

She was blunt, but she was right. "Grace has never needed me, Amy." I cleared my throat before I could go on. "But I need her in my life. I love her. I promise you."

Amy's grin was wide. "Then go get her." She pointed toward the door.

Right on, Amy. I jumped up and looked at my parents. "I gotta go to them."

"Go!" Dad grabbed my keys off the counter and tossed them my way.

"Bring them back with you," Mom called out.

Landon jogged after me. He leaned into the open door as I started my truck. "Now you know, man."

I waited. Waited for him to call me a hypocrite. A pussy. Any of which would be true.

"You know what it feels like to meet the one." He grinned, and I couldn't keep the smile off my face. "Now tell her that." He slammed my door, and I gunned my engine, tires peeling as I flew down the road.

I was going to get my girl and my little dude too.

chapter
Twenty

Grace

Dear Gracie,

Where do we start? Too much time has gone by because of our stubborn pride. I guess we start with sorry. We are so sorry for the way we treated you when you told us you were pregnant. Josh had just died, and I'd like to say that our behavior was due to shock. But that wouldn't be the truth. We were embarrassed. We had high hopes that our perfect child would never make a mistake.

That wasn't fair. That isn't being a parent, and it certainly isn't how God wanted us to treat our family.

We've been praying over what to do. We've asked our pastor, and we've seen a family therapist. We all agree that we made a horrible mistake. We don't want to show up on your doorstep unannounced and ask for forgiveness because you have a child. We have a grandchild. And we don't want to upset him or her.

So we are asking you to contact us. Come to the house. Pick up the phone. Write back. Anything to let us know we can see you. We know that the path to forgiveness will be a long one, but we would like to start. We would like to meet our grandchild.

We love you, Gracie. Even when we acted in the most un-loving way, we never stopped loving you.

Love,

Mom and Dad

I read the damn letter for the twentieth time and then crumpled it into a ball. I threw it in the trash before I could read it again. The coffeemaker beeped, and I sighed in relief. I poured a mug full and wrapped my hands around the warm cup. This was the first contact my parents had tried to make in five years. *They were sorry. They were wrong. They loved me. They wanted to meet Finn.* I was so furious. I was so heartbroken. I was so... confused.

Loving Dean and feeling like, even for a minute, Finn and I were part of a bigger family had made me realize what I was missing. I lost Dean, but maybe, just maybe, I could have my family back. Could I ever forgive them?

"Hiya, Mama!" Finn bounded into the kitchen and sat at the table with a grin. "Merry Christmas Eve!"

"Merry Christmas Eve to you too!" I poured him a bowl of cheerios and added milk and a sliced banana.

"Thank you. Did Joe make you a good cup today?" Despite my emotions from the letter, I giggled. When Finn learned that people sometimes called coffee a cup of Joe, he immediately named our coffeemaker Joe. Finn was the absolute best part of every day.

"Joe did an excellent job." I placed his bowl in front of him and refilled my cup of Joe.

I didn't have a choice when my parents told me to leave. But I had never reached out again. I had never tried to see if they could forgive me or if I could forgive them. We had been at a standoff, and the biggest loser in that standoff was my son. And Finn deserved more than to suffer at the hands of my pride. Finn deserved a family.

Reaching into the trash can, I dug the letter out, smoothed it down, and reread it.

"HO, HO, HO, ho ho!" Finn sang as he hung a Santa ornament on our small tree. Immediately after, he sang along with the holiday song that played on our radio.

I wanted to join him, but I couldn't find the energy. Even three cups of Joe didn't liven me up. I wasn't sure if it was from the letter, my illness, or the loss of Dean, but I couldn't shake my funk. Not even on Christmas Eve.

I sat on the couch, wrapped in a blanket, and handed Finn one ornament at a time from our box. We didn't have a ton, but over the years we had collected some store-bought ornaments from places we had visited and quite a few handmade ones.

"Here's the last one. Then we can hang the popcorn string." I handed Finn a wreath with a picture of his face glued to the center. He put that together in school with Amy this year.

Looking at our tree, I held back my smile. The top third of the tree was bare. Other years, this would have bothered me. I would have subtly moved ornaments around and filled the tree evenly. This year I couldn't bring myself to care.

I was determined that Finn wouldn't suffer from my mood though. We baked cookies, I wrapped his presents, and we watched all the Christmas television shows and movies together. I steeled my heart and tried to think only about Finn.

I was failing, but he didn't notice. His attention was on the happiest time of the year for a child.

Homemade spaghetti sauce, my mom's Christmas Eve tradition, bubbled away on the stove. Three times today I had picked up the phone to call her only to hang up before I dialed. But it was a start. Perhaps it was time to see if forgiveness was in our future.

I heard a knock on my door, and my heart swelled. Did Sylvie cancel her trip? It had to be her or Amy.

Finn followed me to the door, wrapping his body around my leg. I opened it a crack, but all I could see was a huge poinsettia plant.

"Merry Christmas, you two. May I come in?" Dean lowered the plant, and his eyes were soft, his brows drawn together. The sound of his voice alone melted the steel around my heart just a bit, and I opened the door wider.

Finn didn't respond. He turned and walked to the tree, staring at the colored lights in silence. Dean's face fell.

"What are you doing on campus? Shouldn't you be home with your family?" I tucked my hands into the sleeves of my sweatshirt so that I wouldn't reach for him.

"I am home." He stared at me, and both of our eyes filled with tears. "I have so much to say to you." He looked over to Finn. "But first I need to apologize to him."

He handed me the big red plant and a bottle of sparkling cider. *He remembered.*

"Just Finn?" He knelt down next to Finn, but Finn refused to turn his way. "I owe you a big apology." Finn stayed forward, but I saw his chin quiver.

"When I left you said I cracked your heart. I never meant to do that." Dean looked up at Finn and then over to me. "I never wanted to hurt either of your hearts."

Finn's chin and lower lip wobbled. "Can you forgive me? I made a mistake." Finn took in a shaky breath, and Dean turned to me. "Your mommy thought I lied. I didn't lie to either of you. I never will. I should have fought harder. I should have stayed until I made things right. Can you both forgive me for leaving?

I'll have to leave for football a lot in the future, but I never want either of you to feel sad when I'm gone. I always want to come back to you both. Always, Grace. I love you. I love you both so much."

Tears ran down my face. I couldn't keep my feet from moving toward Dean. I knelt in front of him and took his hands in mine. "I love you, Dean. But..."

"Don't say it. Don't even say the words out loud. Jon was wrong. That is not what I said. I never could."

The chill that had permeated my bones for the past two weeks lifted. Warmth filled me. *He did want Finn in his life. He wasn't like... them.*

Dean took Finn's hand in one of his, holding mine in the other. "I want to be a part of this family. If you both will let me."

Finn turned and looked at Dean. "You love me? Like a friend or like a... daddy?"

A sob escaped from my lips before I could control it. Dean's face twisted, and he pulled Finn onto his lap. "I'm not your daddy, little dude. But I love you like you were my son. Does that make sense?"

Finn nodded and wrapped his arms around Dean's neck. "I love you too, Dean. Please don't leave again angry. Mama got sick, and I was scared. I wanted you."

A strangled sound came from Dean's throat, and he squeezed his eyes shut. "I didn't know, little dude. I didn't know your mama was so sick. If I had I would have been here. That will never happen again." He rubbed Finn's back, and Finn lifted his head and kissed Dean's cheek.

Dean blew out a long breath. "Can I talk to your mama alone? We'll be in the kitchen. Can you give us a few minutes?"

Finn nodded. "I'll watch another Christmas show." He turned on Clark Kent and sat cross-legged in front of it. "Go ahead and make up. I'll be right here."

My laughter and tears blended together. He was one smart

little guy. Dean stood up and pulled me along with him. We walked into the kitchen and waited until we heard Finn's show begin.

"I'm sorry—"

"Red, I'm so—"

We spoke at the same time and then stopped together. Dean smiled. "You go first."

"I believed Jon when he told me you wished Finn wasn't in my life." My heart raced in my chest, but I didn't feel weak anymore. I wanted to say this to Dean. I wanted him to understand why I broke up with him. "I think I feared that all along. So when he said it, I snapped. I didn't think it could be untrue or misconstrued. You see, my parents and Josh wished that. And they left me." I gasped and pressed my hands to my chest, pushing hard to take away the jagged pains. "I thought if you felt the same way, even just a little, and if you left Finn and me, even if not in the same way Josh did... you see, it's not just me anymore... I have to look out for Finn's heart too." I walked closer to Dean but stopped before my body touched his.

Dean grunted. He lifted his hand and ran his fingers through my hair, grasping my head. "When Jon told me what he said to you, I almost lost it. The asshole thought he was protecting Finn and helping me. He told me that he talked to you a bit about how he grew up?"

I rolled my neck, nuzzling my head against his hand. The feel of his hand against my head made me feel warm all over. "He told me about his mom and the guys she dated that never stuck around."

Dean's thumb traced the edge of my jaw. "There's more to tell, but that's his story. Regardless, he should have stayed out of our business. I want you to know that I did have a conversation with him where I said that a child in a relationship makes it more difficult. More complicated."

My body tensed, and Dean crouched to look straight into

my eyes. "And then I said I didn't mind complicated for a second. And I don't. My life has been richer and more fun and happier since I met you two than ever before. I want to be a part of this family. I don't want to change one thing. This is where I belong, Red." He dragged his nose along the side of mine. "If you'll have me."

I closed my eyes and absorbed his words. "I love you, Dean."

He tucked me into his side, wrapping his arms around me. "I love you so fucking much, Red. I don't want you to have to be strong all by yourself anymore. I want to be strong together. Understand what I'm saying?"

"Mmmmm." His scent enveloped me, but as good as he smelled, I wanted to taste him more than I wanted to breathe at that moment. "I understand. Now please kiss me." I brought my lips to his, and Dean met me, mouth open, and tongue stroking mine. I held on to his waist and poured every bit of my heart into that kiss. Our teeth banged, our lips molded, and our tongues tangled. The kiss deepened, and Dean moved back, panting.

"We can't. Just Finn. Later. More. Need you." He sounded like an out-of-breath caveman.

I laughed. "Yes, later." Right now a hug would have to suffice. I wrapped my arms around him and held him to me.

Dean kissed the top of my head. "Come home with me tomorrow. I need you to meet the rest of my family," he whispered into my hair.

My heart felt full at his words. He wanted us to be a part of his family. I raised my head up and kissed his jaw. "I would love that. We both would." I snuggled deeper into him.

"What's your favorite part about Christmas?" he asked.

With my cheek pressed against his chest, I relaxed from the rhythm of his powerful, steady heartbeat. "Watching Finn open presents from Santa. What's yours?"

"Sleeping under the tree. I did it every night until I left for college. Can we put Finn to bed and sleep under the tree? I want to hold you… and love you all night."

I turned my face and placed a kiss over his heart. "Thank you."

"For what?"

I looked into the blue eyes that had come to mean so much to me. "For understanding. For coming back. For loving us."

"That's the thing, Red. I'm a stubborn asshole. Once I'm in, I'm in. That's just how it's going to be from now on. The three of us."

Those pesky tears welled up again. "The three of us." They were my favorite words ever spoken.

SPAGHETTI AND SPARKLING cider were consumed. Cookies and milk were laid out by the balcony door, being that I was without the traditional fireplace. Stories were read. As soon as Finn was asleep, cookies were nibbled, and milk was drunk. I placed Finn's presents under the tree while Dean made us a bed of blankets and pillows.

"That's a decent haul of presents, Red." Dean pulled me down next to him on the blanket bed. "How'd you manage to do all that?"

I pointed to a pile of presents wrapped in dancing Santa paper. "Those are all from Sylvie. She spoils Finn every year. The rest are from Santa. Santa saves all year for this. Santa shops at consignment stores, and Santa wraps everything possible individually so there will be more to open. Last year money was really tight, and Santa even wrapped his socks separately." I laughed, but Dean frowned. "What?"

"I don't have presents for either of you. I stopped at the grocery store for the plant and cider. I spaced on gifts." Dean's eyes narrowed. He looked so cute when he was irritated with himself.

I climbed onto his lap and wrapped my legs around his waist. My fingers tangled in his hair. "Are you serious right now?" I kissed the stubble along the bottom of his jaw. "You left your family on Christmas Eve to be with us." I kissed his cheek and then the corner of his mouth. "You apologized to both of us for leaving when I was the one who made you go. You are my gift." I kissed the opposite corner of his mouth and then ran my tongue along his bottom lip. "But there is one other thing I'd like from you this Christmas."

"What's that, baby?" Dean rasped out.

"You." I pressed myself against his hardness. I had never been so sure of anything in my life. "Make love to me tonight. I want you, Dean."

His eyes flared, and he flipped me over so that I was underneath his embrace. "I'll give you anything you want."

He crashed his mouth against mine, our tongues sliding together. He pulled my shirt off, and I yanked his over his head. Two seconds later my bra was unclasped and tossed across the room. We settled, chest to chest, and skin to skin. He bent down, sucking on my breasts, running his tongue over my nipples until I pulled at his hair. My body sang, every nerve ending alive. My heart raced with anticipation.

I unbuttoned his jeans, pulling them off as he unbuttoned and unzipped mine. Our lips stayed fused, our hands hurried, as we rid ourselves of the last of our clothes.

It was time. We were ready.

His fingers caressed me, circling and rubbing as I moved beneath him. "Please, now. Please," I begged. My body had never been so ready before.

His grin was sexy as hell. He reached over to his jeans and pulled a condom from his wallet. He moved fast, ripping open the package and rolling it onto himself. I was glad he hadn't asked me to do that. My hands shook, and my excitement made me giddy.

Dean propped himself up on his elbows, eyes glued to mine. "I love you, Grace. Thank you for letting me get to love you. I'm so damn lucky."

I couldn't hold back a grin as my eyes filled with happy tears. He slid inside me, inch by inch, and I gasped. I felt every minute of the five years that had passed since I had been with a guy. Those times as a teenager were uncertain, unsure, and unskilled. Being with Dean, someone who had more experience than I wanted to think about but also had confidence and a steady and sure adoration of me, was unparalleled. He moved above me, lifting my hips and helping me find a rhythm that sent a building sensation rushing through me.

Somewhere in the distance I heard my voice chant Dean's name. His eyes never left mine, hooded, dark, and heated. I ran my hands up his back, slick with sweat, and over his arms, taut and tense as he held himself up.

I felt like I was in a tunnel, dark and narrow until the world exploded around me in bursts of color. He swallowed my sounds with his mouth as I came, and I allowed my body to indulge in every second of the pleasure I felt.

I had no clue. None.

Sex with the man that I loved with an earth-shattering ferocity was mind-blowing.

"Grace, my God. Grace." I couldn't tear my eyes from Dean. His jaw set, his eyes narrowed into slants, and I watched as he stilled, threw his head back and groaned, his orgasm overtaking him.

He collapsed onto me. I wrapped myself around him, arms and legs and body and soul. He was mine. I would love him forever. I knew that in the same way I knew the sky was blue.

We held each other in silence, catching our breath and stroking our sweaty skin for a long time. Dean ran his hands up and down my back, and I pressed kisses to his chest. Finally we pulled away, and lay side by side on our backs, only the lights from the Christmas tree illuminating the room.

"I don't want this night to end. I don't want to leave this apartment." He kissed my lips. "But I have to. Just know in the coming months when you need me, I'm here."

I wrapped my arms around his neck. "I have two favorite guys in this world now. Two gifts. Merry Christmas, Dean."

"Best night of my life, baby. Merry Christmas, Red."

chapter
Twenty-One

Dean

"OKAY, REMIND ME of everyone's names one more time."
Grace pulled on her fingers, knotting and unknotting them.

I looked in the rearview mirror. Finn was still asleep. He
had woken us up at the crack of dawn, jumping onto our blanket
bed and screaming out, "Merry Christmas!"

Finn tore through his presents like a man on a mission. He
had new books, movies, trucks, dinosaurs, and of course, superheroes. With Amy's assistance, Finn had bought a few gifts for
Grace. Perfume and a homemade coupon book made Grace so
happy. I didn't quite get the concept of a homemade coupon
book until I paged through. Grace could choose from free hugs,
kisses, breakfast in bed, no complaining toy pickups, table setting, and more. It was pretty fucking cute.

After a pancake breakfast, we piled into the car to head to
my parents' home. Grace was uncomfortable that she didn't have
a gift for them, so I convinced her to give them the poinsettia.
She agreed but with little enthusiasm.

"Devin, Dianna, Damian, Daisy, and Delilah. In that order. I'm the oldest, tallest, and most good-looking." I winked, and her returning smile was small. "Red, they're gonna love you. They're going to tease me. That's just what they do, but they will love you."

She blew out a breath. "How do you know?"

"I know because I love you. I've never brought a girl home from college. They're going to be curious about you but also excited. They're huge pains in the asses, but they're my family." I took her hand in mine and squeezed.

Grace looked over her shoulder at Finn. "I have to tell you something about my family. My parents."

I tightened the grip of my hand on the steering wheel. Her parents were assholes. But they were still her family.

"My mom sent me a Christmas card and a letter asking me to come home and let them apologize. She said they didn't want to show up at my apartment with my child there without my permission."

She paused, and I waited. This was huge for her.

"I'm considering stopping by the house. Not with Finn, of course, but maybe with... you? Would you come with me?" Grace studied my profile as I watched the road.

I loosened my grip. If I was with her, I could protect her. "Hell yes. You're not going alone, I'll tell you that right now. And if they hurt you..." I shut up before I said too much. Turning left, I pulled my truck into my driveway.

Grace squeezed my hand. "I know. I'll be okay." She leaned over and kissed my cheek. "I have you, after all."

I put the car into park. "Baby." I cupped her face and kissed her lips. From the front door, even with the windows closed and engine running, I could hear the hoots and hollering of my siblings. "You have me and my annoying family. C'mon."

I took the key out of the ignition and jumped out of the truck. Reaching into the backseat for Finn, I lifted him into my arms. He woke, still drowsy, and wrapped his body around mine. As I rounded the truck, I took Grace's hand and we walked up the path.

"Move back, you pack of dogs." My dad's gruff voice was welcome. My siblings scattered and my parents met us at the door. "Welcome to our home, Grace and Finn." Grace extended her hand, and my dad beamed. "Gotta hug you, girl. You tamed my beast of a son. That's gonna get you a hug." My dad pulled Grace into his embrace. She giggled, and I relaxed.

"Grace." Mom pulled Grace from my father. "We're so happy that you and your son are here. Are you feeling better?" Mom held Grace's hands in each of hers, pulling Grace's arms to the sides as she inspected her.

"I'm much better, thank you, Mrs. Goldsmith." Grace's cheeks turned pink, and I bit back my grin.

"Oh no!" Mom made a clucking sound, tucking her bent elbow around Grace's arm. She led her into the family room. "Call me Dorothy. And that old man is Dale."

Grace nodded and looked over her shoulder at Finn and me. I winked, and her returning smile was the best Christmas gift I could have been given.

"Dad, this is Finn." Finn lifted his sleepy head from my shoulder and waved.

"Hello there, young man. Welcome. You need anything, you ask me. I'm the big kahuna around here." He rumpled Finn's hair, and Finn laughed. We walked into the family room, and I groaned.

My sisters and brothers had signage.

Each stood in a row holding up a piece of white poster board. Delilah was first. She laughed uncontrollably as she yelled out her greeting. "Welcome, Dean's friends! We hope you know what you're getting into! Here's a preview."

Flipping her sign to the front, she read aloud what was printed in neat black block lettering:

Dean told me I was adopted.
And a boy.
I believed him.
For three years!!!!

She peered around the sign. "I'm Delilah! I'm fifteen!"

I couldn't help but laugh. First off, there was no doubt that all the Goldsmiths were related. We looked like clones. Second, of all my sisters she was the girliest. Petite with light blond hair, blue eyes, and the longest eyelashes I'd ever seen. How had I pulled that off for three years? That prank was still my favorite.

Grace looked back at me with her lips pressed together. She turned back to my youngest sibling. "I'm Grace, and this is my son, Finn. He's four." Delilah waved.

Finn looked around the room and buried his face in my neck. I wanted to bury my face too. This place was overwhelming to me, and I grew up here. My parents' family room was filled with a gigantic tree, presents underneath, stockings overflowing with candy, holiday music playing, a fire in the fireplace, and my goofy siblings. Holding signs. *Jesus.*

Daisy raised her sign next and read in a loud, proud voice.

Dean sprays us girls with mountain-scented air freshener before dates to keep the boys away. Doesn't work! Ha!

She lowered her sign and spoke to Grace. "It's true. Before every date whenever he's home. He's such a tool." She blew me a kiss. "I'm Daisy, and I'm seventeen!"

Grace turned around, her mouth open. "You really do that?"

I nodded, grinning. "Look at them. They share my genes. They're good-looking chicks. Boys need to stay away."

My dad held up his hand. I high-fived him. Dad was too old for a fist bump.

"Nothing says unattractive like smelling like pine. It's not hot." I shrugged, and Delilah threw a pillow at my head. It bounced off Finn's back, and he raised his head.

"Hey," he protested, and Delilah's smug grin fell.

"I'm sorry, Finn. I was aiming for my brother." She stuck out her lower lip in a pout like she always did to get out of trouble.

Finn wrapped his arms around my shoulders. "Be nice to my Dean. I love him."

A chorus of "awws" went up around the room.

"My turn." Damian held up his sign.

He'll eat the last donut/piece of cake/pie/muffin/cookie. Every time. He's a hog. Oink, oink.

Damian snorted as he finished reading, and the room erupted in more laughter. Grace joined right in.

"I'm a growing boy." I shrugged again. None of this was a lie.

Damian moved his sign to the floor. He dragged a hand through his shaggy blond hair. "I'm Damian by the way. The hot one. I'm eighteen."

Grace muffled her giggle with her hand. I shot my brother the bird behind Finn's back. Hot one, my ass.

The twins were next. Their signs were behind their backs. This would suck. They knew the most. Dianna spoke up. "We're the twins, Devin and Dianna. We're twenty and attend Purdue."

"Boooooo." I heckled them, but they only smirked in return. *Shitballs*. Dianna raised her sign.

He wet the bed until he was nine. One time he peed in his own closet when he was sleepwalking. PROTECT YOUR SHOES!

The room was going wild. Daisy and Damian fell onto the floor laughing. Grace turned around again wide-eyed. "Did you really wet the bed until you were nine?"

"Yup. Sorry again, Mom." Mom was wiping the tears from her eyes, enjoying this show way too much. I considered retracting said apology.

Finn jerked up. "Ewwww," he said as his little lips pinched

together with a frown.

"Last, but never least." Devin flipped his sign around. It was simple but poignant.

Meet Woobie the Boobie.

No fucking way. He wouldn't...

He did. Devin reached behind him and pulled out Woobie. My siblings were screaming with laughter. Even my father clutched his side from laughing too hard.

"Seems like our Dean here was always a boob man. Mom couldn't get him off the teat, so she stuffed this tan sock and sewed it shut. Told him it was his very own boobie to sleep with. This tool named it Woobie. Know where I found it?" Devin asked Grace.

She shook her head, her face bright red.

"In his bed. He STILL sleeps with his Woobie when he comes home!" Devin doubled over in laughter.

"That's not true!" It really was. I don't know, my ma made it for me. And, it was a boob... I coughed away my own laughter. "Where's the loyalty, bro?"

"I tried to take it from him many times," Mom said, gasping for air.

Grace tugged on my arm. "Is that..." She gasped for breath. "a...?"

Mom jumped in. "It is! The top part is red to look just like a nipple. He insisted!"

"I'm going to pee my pants," Delilah yelled out.

Grace waved her hand in front of her face. "I'm sorry, Dean. This is so funny. Disturbing, but funny."

That set off another round of laughter. Finn jumped down from my arms and walked over to Grace. He slipped his hand into hers. "I like them, Mama."

That quieted them down. The laughter stopped, and my siblings looked at Finn and then at me. They were happy for me. The Goldsmiths just showed it in unique ways.

"It's a pleasure to meet all of you. Thank you for sharing your Christmas with my son and me." Grace walked over and hugged each of them. Finn followed, shaking hands.

"Sit down, sit down. Time for presents! We waited for you to arrive!" Mom clapped her hands and shooed us all to our seats.

Devin slipped me an envelope, and I joined Grace on the couch.

"Our tradition is to pass gifts around and open them at the same time. Okay?" Mom asked Grace.

Grace's face reddened. "I'm so sorry, but I didn't know we were coming. I don't have any gifts for you. We'll just watch, Finn." Finn nodded, and my mom bit her lip. She was up to something.

I elbowed Grace. "You got Mom a present. Mom, we have a big ol' poinsettia in the truck for you." I grinned as Grace rolled her eyes.

Dad handed out the gifts, giving one to Finn and one to Grace last.

"What is this?" Grace whispered.

"Mom? How did you…?"

Daisy stood up and wrapped an arm around my mom's waist. "She shopped on Christmas Eve, just like the rest of us. Probably killed her to be a last-minute shopper, but she's over-the-moon excited you both are here."

Mom clasped her hands in front of her chest. "Welcome to our family, Grace. If Dean loves you, we know we all will."

A tear rolled down Grace's face, and she nodded. "Thank you so much. The feeling is mutual."

We opened present after present. Mom had an equal number for everyone, even for Grace and Finn. My mom fucking rocked.

Once the pile under the tree was empty, I stood up. "I want to thank Mom and Dad for being so awesome. You both are more generous than any of us deserve." I pulled the envelope from Devin out of my back pocket. "I had to call in some favors from my brother on this one, but he got the purchases made and papers printed. Thanks, man."

Devin lifted his chin, and I handed Grace the envelope.

She opened it, and her jaw dropped. "No. No." She looked up at me. "Dean!"

"Yes, Red. You deserve this and more." I knelt in front of Finn. "I play in my last college bowl game on New Year's Day. For your Christmas present, I got you and your mom plane tickets to see me in the game. You'll fly down on the twenty-ninth, and we have tickets to go to Disney World the next day."

Finn jumped up. "A plane! I've never been on a plane!" He hugged me and then Grace. "And Mickey? I get to see Mickey the mouse?" His grin was huge, and his voice got louder and higher pitched with each word. I nodded, and he leaped into my arms again.

"Mama?" He turned back to Grace, who was busy wiping away her tears. "The best part is that we get to see Dean play again. I'm gonna cheer so loud he'll hear me this time. I know it."

"I will, little dude. I totally will hear you."

I looked around at my family, and I saw it in each person's expression. They knew why I loved Grace and Finn. And they would fall in love with them too. That in and of itself was the greatest gift I could give Grace and Finn. The love and loyalty of the Goldsmith clan was loud, often obnoxious, but never ending.

chapter
Twenty-Two

Grace

DEAN AND I crept out of his old room and walked into the kitchen. "He's finally asleep. He didn't want to leave your brothers and sisters. He's had the best day." I kissed Dean's lips, and he held me against him.

"I need a minute alone with you. Then we can join the others." His lips moved against mine, and he slipped his tongue into my mouth. I moaned and sucked on his tongue for a second.

"You better cut that out," he spoke against my lips. "Don't start something you can't finish, Red."

"Oh, I can finish and quietly I might add. You? You're pretty much a beast, so staying quiet is not gonna happen." He growled, and I giggled, kissing him chastely. "Thank you for bringing me here." I wrapped my arms around his waist, and we held each other.

"Knock, knock."

We pulled back as a side door into Dean's kitchen opened. A tall, built guy with brown hair walked in. He held hands with a short, petite blonde. She held the door open, and in walked Amy.

"Amy!" I ran over, and we hugged. "I'm so happy to see you."

"Hi, Grace! I am glad you and Dean made up. That makes me smile." Amy did just that as Dean walked over.

"Amy." Dean paused and looked at me before turning back to her. "Thank you for talking to me yesterday and helping me get my head on straight. If it weren't for you, I wouldn't have my girl and my little dude back."

Amy placed a hand on Dean's shoulder. "Now do not be a dickhead again, okay?"

Dean threw his head back in laughter. Amy looked at me wide-eyed. "I was serious." We all laughed harder at that.

"Grace, I'm Emma, and this is Landon. We're friends with Dean and Amy. It's so nice to meet you."

I shook their hands. "I've heard a lot about both of you from Dean and Amy."

"Is it safe for me to join you all?" Jon poked his head in the doorway. "I come in peace." He held up a case of beer.

"C'mon in." Dean wasn't friendly, but he was polite. He held my hand tightly in his, and some of the tension I felt around Jon dissipated.

Jon placed the beer on the table. "Grace, I owe you a big apology. I should never have gotten into your and Dean's relationship. I turned my past crap into worry about Finn. That was wrong. You aren't my mom and Dean isn't those guys. I'm sorry." He held out his hand, and we shook.

If anyone understood baggage from their childhood, it was me. "Apology accepted. But I believe you came from a place of good intentions, Jon." I smiled, and he blew out a breath.

"Still gonna deck you," Dean rumbled out.

Jon nodded. "I know that. I'll take it when it comes. Until then, have a beer with me." He tossed a can at Dean, and he caught it, popping it open and taking a large drink.

We settled around the table, beers for most and soda for some.

"Where's Ricardo?" Landon asked Jon.

Jon shrugged, but his eyebrows pulled together. "Something's going on with him. He won't answer my texts. I stopped by his house, and he wasn't there either."

Landon and Dean exchanged worried looks. "I'll try to catch up with him tomorrow," Landon announced, and Dean seemed to relax at this.

Two hours later I felt like a part of the group. Dean and Landon teased one another mercilessly. Emma attempted to tamp down the crude jokes, and Amy laughed along with everyone.

After Dorothy's huge Christmas lunch, I didn't think I could ever eat again, but that was not the case for anyone else. Dorothy had two huge pots of chili on the stove, and people moved in and out of the kitchen, filling bowls and adding toppings. Like Dean, his siblings had a stream of friends coming in and out of the house. Everyone was welcome, with Dale and Dorothy moving around, joining different groups. I wondered what it would be like to grow up like this, with lots of siblings, friends, and with parents who were open and loving.

I wanted all of that for Finn. For the first time I thought he might get it.

"Dean filled us in on your background, Grace. I'm sorry to hear about all of your losses. Unfortunately, Landon has had a similar issue with his parents. Have you reached out to yours since Finn was born?" Emma sat on Landon's lap, their fingers entwined.

I looked at Dean. "No." I shifted to face Emma. "But just today I told Dean that they sent me a letter asking me to contact them. As mad as I am at them, I still miss them. They're my parents."

Emma looked into Landon's eyes for a long moment. He nodded, and she kissed his lips.

"I'm—" Landon cleared his throat. "I'm thinking of contacting mine too. Emma and I have been talking about it, and with moving back home next summer, I know I'll need to smooth things over." He looked at Emma. "I mean, I want to move on. Emma and I will have a family together someday. I need my stuff sorted before then."

I nodded, ripping the napkin in front of me into pieces. "I know what you mean. I'm not sure I can ever forgive them, but I have a family, and my son deserves to know his grandparents."

Landon met my eyes, and the ball of tension inside me eased. He understood where I was coming from. Dean tried, but with a family like he had, he would never fully understand the feeling of abandonment when your parents turned their backs on you. No matter how old you were when that happened, it was a pain that was hard to describe.

Daisy walked into the kitchen and grabbed a bottle of water from the refrigerator. She was stunning. Taller, like her older brother, but curvier than her other sisters. Her chest filled out her snug, long-sleeved white T-shirt, and her ripped jeans clung to her hips. Daisy had a woman's body even at the age of seventeen. Long, white-blond hair hung straight down her back, and she shared the same crystal-blue eyes that all of the Goldsmith siblings were blessed with.

"Merry Christmas everybody!" Daisy greeted our group, propping a hip against the kitchen counter.

Everyone greeted her back, but Jon caught my attention. He stared at Daisy with a strange intensity. I really hoped Dean missed it.

"Are you checking out my little sister?" Dean bellowed at Jon and smacked the back of his head.

Landon burst out laughing as Jon rubbed the back of his head. "No, man. Chill out."

Daisy cringed and then blushed. "Thanks, Dean. Always an asshole." She turned on her heel and left the kitchen.

Dean cracked the knuckles on each of his hands. "Stay away from my sisters, man-slut," he spoke in a low warning voice to Jon.

Jon tightened his jaw but said nothing. I thought that a wise move myself.

"Dean, do you leave for Orlando soon?" Landon asked, in a much-needed subject change. He rubbed Emma's back as she snuggled against him.

"Yeah." He looked my way and frowned. "Day after tomorrow. They want us there a few days early to acclimate and practice. Grace and Finn come a few days later, and we're doing Disney."

"Oooo! I love Disney World! You have to buy Finn mouse ears." Amy spoke with excitement.

"Anything he wants," Dean answered Amy. "Then after the senior bowl game at the end of January, I'm off to train in Arizona before the Scouting Combine. After the combine I'll be crazy too."

"Right. Training and stuff with your agent?" Jon piped in, popping the top on another beer.

Dean sat back and folded his hands behind his head. "That's just the tip of it—"

"That's what she said!" Jon and Landon yelled in unison. Emma and I groaned, and Amy narrowed her eyes, looking at Emma and then at me.

"Ignore them." I hoped to distract her from the double birdies Dean was waving at his friends.

Dean stood up and filled a bowl with chili. "I've got meetings about endorsements, face-to-faces with coaches. Tons of shit going on." He moved back to the table and kissed the top of my head. "Gonna miss my Red and her Finn."

"You do your thing. I'm working on graduating this spring. Amy will be there to help me with Finn." I looked over, and Amy's face had erupted in an ear-to-ear smile. "We'll be here when you have time. Don't worry about us."

He leaned forward and brushed his lips against mine. "Always worry, baby."

I felt my face burn. With embarrassment, with love, with passion.

I burned for him.

THE DRIVE TO Noblesville took less than forty minutes. I spent that time clutching one of Dean's large hands in both of mine. We listened to music and discussed the trip to Florida. Dean was trying to distract me, but nothing could take my mind off seeing my parents for the first time in five years.

Dorothy and Dale were watching Finn for the morning. They had asked to take him to a movie, and his leap in the air was all the affirmation they needed. I trusted that he was in good hands, and that was at least one less worry on my mind.

The house looked the same. I grew up in a small brick rancher with a white front porch. Through the bay window lights from their Christmas tree twinkled. My mom liked to decorate the outside of the house, but there was nothing festive there today.

Dean parked along the side of the road and turned off the engine. "You sure about this?" I continued to clutch his hand in mine. With his other hand he tucked a lock of hair behind my ear.

"Yes." I cleared my throat. "I need to do this."

"Okay, Red." Dean brushed his lips against mine. "Just remember, whatever they say, you're loved. If they choose not to give you theirs, they're the stupidest fuckers in the world. But if that happens, I'll just double mine."

"Dean." I closed my eyes and forced back my tears. "I love

you."

"I love you, baby." He kissed me again before he pulled away and got out of the truck. He came around and opened my door, and I hopped down into his arms. We hugged, and I soaked up his love and strength and confidence before we walked up the drive.

I knocked on the pale-blue painted door and held my breath. My mom was a homemaker, so unless she was at the store, she'd answer. My dad was a mechanic, so I doubted he would be home the day after a holiday.

The door opened, and my mom stared back at me. She looked so much older. Her short hair was streaked with gray, and her face was wrinkled in places where it had been smooth. She looked thinner, wearing faded blue jeans and a plaid button-down shirt.

Mom looked at Dean and then again at me. Her face crumpled, and she covered it with her hands. "You're here. You came back. Gracie," she sobbed into her hands.

"Can we talk?" I asked, and Dean wrapped an arm around my shoulder.

Mom removed her hands from her face and wiped under her red eyes. "Of course, I'm sorry. I'm so rude. Please." She ushered us into the house "Please, come in and sit down."

We sat up straight on the faded plaid couch, Dean's leg pressing against my own. Dean's arms rested on the top of his legs, his hands clasped together. He looked on edge and ready to protect at a moment's notice.

I could have done this by myself. I was independent and capable, but the fact was, I was so glad I didn't have to do it alone. Dean was my blessing, and I wanted him with me.

"Can I get either of you a drink? Your father's at work." Mom spoke rapidly. She pulled on her fingers, wringing her hands together.

I got it. I was scared too.

"No, thank you." Dean's voice was low and while not rude, was not friendly either.

I shook my head. "Mom, please sit down. We won't stay long."

Mom sat down on the edge of the chair across from us. "No, don't rush. Take your time."

"I—" I looked at Dean and then at my mom. "I'm not really sure where to start." I swallowed and took a deep breath. "I got your letter asking me to come here. Was this about my son?"

Mom jolted back. "You have a son?" Her fingers covered her open mouth.

"Finn. Finn Joshua Yeates." Dean grasped my hand in his, holding it tight. "He's the best, Mom. He's funny and sweet and loves superheroes—" Mom held up her hand, palm facing me, and I stopped talking.

"I can't hear this. Not until I say what I need to say." Mom stood up and walked to the sliding glass door that led to our tiny backyard. "We were so wrong. We judged you and told you not to... to... have him. That was horrible." She walked over and knelt beside me. She placed her hands on my knees, and I could feel her body shaking. "All because we feared what other people would think of us, having a daughter who got pregnant out of wedlock. Our fear of judgment caused us to lose our only daughter. Judgment is the biggest sin of all, Gracie. I need to ask, no... no. I need to *beg* for your forgiveness."

Tears rolled down her face, but mine hadn't fallen yet. My body was too tightly wound. My heart was too steeled. I hadn't expected this. I never thought she would beg for absolution.

"Then why, Mom? Why if you regret telling me to leave have you stayed away all this time? Why didn't you come to see me? We've been all alone. I've raised Finn ALL BY MYSELF." I shouted the last words, pulling away from Dean and moving past my mom to walk over to those same glass doors. "He's never had a backyard to play in. We live in a campus apartment.

Every single holiday has been spent alone, just the two of us. What I can't wrap my brain around is why you let that stand? Why you didn't fix this before now?"

She wept as she spoke. "Your dad and I fell apart when you left. We convinced ourselves that we were right when we knew in our hearts that we were wrong. We've been alone too. Every holiday it's just been us. We haven't celebrated or gone to parties. We wanted to punish ourselves the way we punished you." She got up and walked next to me. "I prayed and prayed about what to do. I'm sure I was wrong, but I convinced myself that if you were open to forgiving us, you'd come home." She put her hands on my shoulders and moved me to face her. "Finally I decided to stop being a coward and to write you a letter. And you came home. Your heart and your strength brought you back. I will do anything I can to make this up to you. Will you forgive me?"

My tears came. They ran down my face, a first start at releasing the pent-up anger and sadness and pain that I carried toward my parents.

"I'll try. This is the first step. But I'm going to need time, Mama." At the sound of her name, the way I always had addressed her, her knees buckled. I grasped her arms to steady her.

"You called me Mama." She choked back a sob. "That's so precious, Gracie. Thank you."

"Is Dad on the same page?" I was terrified to hear that he wasn't, but I needed to ask.

Mom nodded, wiping her cheeks with the back of her hand. "He wanted to reach out even before I did. After he got over his anger, he was mortified with what we'd done. It took me longer to be ready to say sorry. He'll be heartbroken that he wasn't here. When he hears he has a grandson..." She took a shaky breath. "When can we meet him? I'll wait as long as you need, but I have to apologize to him too."

I held out my hand toward Dean, and he got up and joined

me. "Mom, this is my boyfriend, Dean. We're taking Finn to Florida this week to watch Dean play in his bowl game. After the New Year, Finn and I will be back home in Bloomington. I'll call you and Dad. Maybe you can visit us there?"

Mom nodded furiously. "Anything. Whatever is best for you and Finn." She held out her hand. "Dean, it's nice to meet you. I'm sure you don't like my husband or me right now, but I hope over time to earn your trust too."

Dean didn't smile. He held out his hand and shook my mom's. "I hope so too, Mrs. Yeates." He released her hand and pulled me close to him. "My priorities are Grace and Finn. If they're happy, I'm happy."

Mom's smile was small. "You have your priorities in order then."

I looked at my watch. "Mom, we have to go. Dean's parents took Finn to a movie, and I want to be back when they get home." A flash of pain shot across her face at my words, but she recovered.

"Of course. Thank you, Grace. Thank you so very much." We hugged and left. Just like that. Just like that, I made the first step toward forgiving and fixing the most painful relationship of my life. I couldn't help but think that by opening my hard heart to Dean's love, I allowed the pain to ease and made room for more good.

Dean opened the passenger door to his truck. He lifted me in, and when I was eye level with him, he brought his face closer to mine. "As long as I live, I will never forget what I just saw. You are the most incredible woman in the world, Grace. You're my hero. I'm so damn happy to be able to love you, Red."

He kissed me softly and then deeper. My heart beat faster, and my body relaxed.

I was more than happy to have fallen in love with Dean. I was blessed.

DEAN'S TRUCK PULLED into his parent's driveway at the same time their minivan rounded the corner. We hopped out to meet them, and I bounced on my toes to get warm. Late December in Indiana was brutal. The temperatures were frigid, and the forecast called for snow that evening. Our jackets were in the car, but Dean and I wore thick sweaters. I cupped my hands around my mouth and blew warm air onto them.

Dale parked the minivan next to Dean's truck, and Finn leaped out the side door. He walked over with Dale and Dorothy, an enormous smile stretched across his face.

"Mama, the movie was so good. I laughed and cheered and even got mad at some parts. I ate popcorn and candy and drank root beer. It was the best day ever."

Dean chuckled. "Did my old man behave himself? He's known to steal all the popcorn."

Finn shook his head, his expression serious. "No. He did not steal any. He had his own bag." We all laughed as Dale rubbed his protruding belly.

"Finn was wonderful, dear," Dorothy chimed in. She wrapped her arm around Dale's waist. "This one," she pointed to Dale with her other hand, "got a bit teary at the end."

Dale shot his wife a mock glare. "The daddy dinosaur got hurt. It was sad, and I'm man enough to admit that."

Finn and I giggled along with Dorothy, and Dale joined in. Dean took my hand in his, entwining our fingers together and squeezed.

Finn walked up to us, eyes sparkling with laughter and joy.

"Are you happy, Super Finn? I smiled down at him.

He shook his head. Dorothy and Dale stopped laughing. Finn took Dean and my enjoined hands and pulled our fingertips toward the ground, keeping them pressed together. He slowly moved our palms apart and angled our thumbs down toward the ground still touching at the tips.

He'd made our hands into a heart.

"Not just happy, Mama. My heart is full. My heart is happy."

Dean's father grunted, and I looked over to see Dorothy wiping her eyes. I turned to Dean, but he was focused on Finn. The two most important people in my life smiled at one another, a look of such complete adoration that my own heart swelled.

I'd been given two blessings in my life and with those guys by my side—and with their love in my heart, our future was bright.

chapter
Twenty-Three

Dean

"DO YOU KNOW what we've never done?" I poured more champagne into Grace's glass and then topped off my own.

She took a small sip. "What haven't we done?" Her smile was soft and relaxed.

Organizing a proper Valentine's Day for Grace took some effort. First I had to convince her that Finn was ready for an overnight with my parents. Finn had been asking for weeks, as had my mom and dad, but Grace was unsure. After one of our marathon late-night talks, she agreed. Next I had to fly into Bloomington and meet with Sylvie to make sure Grace's shifts were covered. I had also pleaded with Sylvie to help me shop for clothes and shoes for Grace. Not to mention keeping my plans a surprise for Grace was killing me. I told her everything, but I wanted tonight to be special.

After dropping Finn off with my parents, Grace and I went downtown and checked into our room at the Marriott. As requested, chilled champagne waited for us. Now the difficult part was remembering that we had dinner reservations in an hour. All I wanted at the moment was to fall into bed with Grace and stay there for the next twenty-four hours.

"Ahem? Earth to Dean." Grace nudged my leg with her foot. Her toenails were painted a deep, shiny red.

I closed my slackened mouth, hoping no drool escaped. "Sorry, I was picturing those toes digging into my ass while I'm on top of you later." Grace gasped, her face flushing, and I winked. "I have a lot of plans that involve your body under and on top of mine, Red."

Grace placed her glass on the nightstand and crawled over to me. She took my glass and placed it on the opposite nightstand. "Keep going. Tell me your plans." She climbed onto my lap, straddling me, and ran her fingers—nails also painted red—through my hair. "I have plans too, you know."

Leaning forward, I pressed my lips to hers. "I was going to say we've never made love in a real bed. On your couch, in my truck, and on your floor, but not in an honest-to-God bed." The truck, while visiting my parents over Christmas, was my go-to memory whenever we were separated.

"Don't forget the hotel room closet at Disney." Grace moaned against my lips, pressing our bodies tighter together. God, how did I forget that? I had to sleep in the team block of rooms, but I sure as hell snuck off to her room once Finn was asleep. I was a loud motherfucker, and we quickly realized there was no other choice but the closet. Worked for me.

"Mmm, and the truck." Grace touched her tongue along the outer edge of my ear, and I groaned. "Did you like it when I sat on your lap?" She bit my earlobe and whispered, "When I rode you real good like that?" Her hands undid the buttons on my shirt, and her hips moved against me in a rhythm that mimicked what we did that night along a country road, desperate to be together in private.

"Fuck, Red." My body tensed. I was so damn hard. I hadn't been with her since January. I'd just finished my training for the combine, and although we had mastered phone sex, my hand was no substitute for Grace's lush body. "I've turned you into a bad girl. And I fucking love it." My hips bucked up to meet hers, and she moaned. Her lips found mine, and we kissed long and hard.

Shit. Dinner. I pulled her back, both of us panting. "Baby, dinner reservations are in an hour." I kissed down her throat and along her collarbone. "I bought you a dress and shoes. Let me take you out and feed you. Then I'll come home and take care of you in bed."

She pressed down harder against me. "I can't make it through dinner." She pulled my shirt off my shoulders and tossed it aside. Her top was next, and before I could even participate, her bra was flung onto the ground. "Yes," she hissed when her breasts made contact with my chest.

Fuck dinner. We'd go late or not at all. "That's it." I flipped her onto her back. I kissed her, sucking on her tongue and then her lower lip. I moved down her body, stopping to lick and bite her nipples.

"Dean." She arched her back and ran her hands up my arms and around my shoulders. "Please, I need more."

I grinned around her nipple. I released it and continued my kisses down her body, grabbing her skirt as I went and pulled it off. Grace lay on the bed in her tiny underwear, red, thank Christ. I moved off the bed and yanked my pants and boxers down before coming right back to her.

"I've missed your taste, Red." I placed kisses over the top of her panties, and she writhed, grabbing the sheet with her hands.

She uttered something, but I couldn't understand her. All I heard was the need and desire in her tone. I felt the same. Long-distance relationships sucked, but in the end, I'd make sure we were together, and I'd give her the life she deserved.

I inched the red panties down and off her, and then my lips and tongue found her, right where she ached for me. *For me.* The strongest woman I knew needed something from *me*. Not football, not my family, not my friends, nothing had ever made me feel like more of a man.

My body was strung so tight I thought I might snap. But my time would come. I ran my tongue up and down and then around and around in circles. Grace began to chant my name as she thrashed her head back and forth on the pillow. She kept her eyes open, watching me like I liked.

When her jaw dropped, and she held her breath, I knew she was there. Her low moan almost made me come on my own, but I managed to hold back. I kissed her thighs and belly as I made my way back up to her lips. I moved slowly, allowing her body time to come back down.

She smiled a lazy, satisfied grin. "My turn." Grace sat up and moved onto her knees.

"Nope. No can do." I pulled her back up to me and nuzzled against her neck. "Been too long, baby. I'll be finished in two seconds if you put me in that sweet mouth."

She laughed. "Okay, later then. I miss the taste of you too."

I stilled. "Hell, you can't talk like that to me, baby." I sucked on her lower lip again. "It sounds so good it hurts."

Her hands ran down, and she grasped me. Okay, she was missing how much power she had over my body. I needed inside of her now. NOW.

"Where do you want me?" She moved her hand up and down as I reached for the condom, ripping it open. I lay on my back, and she took it from my hand and rolled it on. I practiced deep breathing exercises and recalled my team's football stats to calm me down.

"You choose," I growled, eyes squeezed shut. I kept them closed as she moved.

"I chose," she said.

When I opened my eyes, she was on all fours, perfect ass lifted into the air. Jesus, Mary, and Joseph, what did I ever do in my life to deserve this?

I sat up and moved onto my knees behind her. "Baby." I ran my hands up the backs of her thighs and circled her ass. "You're perfect." Those were the last intelligible words I spoke as I sank into her. I held on to her hips and controlled my strokes as she moaned and cursed in front of me.

I wasn't lying—it had been too long. I prayed she was as keyed up as I was. She turned her head back, watching me slam into her, and her eyes fluttered closed. She was close. My hands gripped her tighter, and I increased my speed. She came, tightening around me with a yelp. Her head dropped down, and I let myself go.

My groan was loud and long. I draped my body over hers, still joined, and rested my weight on my hands. "You are mine, Red. I'll never get enough of this. Never enough of you." My words were choppy as I caught my breath, still joined with her.

When our heartbeats slowed, we moved and lay side by side, fingers entwined. She turned to face me, drawing circles on my chest with her fingertips. "Still thinking about dinner?" Her teasing tone was too damn cute.

"Baby, I could never eat food again, and I'd die a happy man." I tweaked her nose, and she giggled.

"Dean?"

"Yes, Red?"

"I like beds. Very much."

She licked her lips, and my body revved up for round two. "I like beds, but I love you. Happy Valentine's Day, Grace."

She leaned over and kissed my chest, right over my heart. "This was my favorite one ever. Happy Valentine's Day, Dean."

And it was my favorite one too. Until next year when I'd make sure she had her own big-ass bed to spend it in.

No matter where I was in the future, she and Finn would be with me. And I knew right then that every damn day with them would be my favorite.

Epilogue

Dean

"AND WITH THE fifth draft pick, the Chicago Bears choose… Dean Goldsmith, Indiana University."

This wasn't a surprise. I had gotten off the phone with the Bear's Head Coach a few minutes ago. When I was invited to join the draft, I knew right away that I didn't want to sit in an auditorium, watching the announcements live. That would overwhelm Finn, and besides, I wanted all my friends and family with me. Even Coach K was here, looking as proud as I'd ever seen him.

When the phone call came in, Andrew only grinned. We both had been told this would happen. I would have loved a spot with the Colts, but their quarterback was tenacious. If I wanted to start, I had to go where I was needed. The best thing about Chicago was that it was close to home.

Not that I wouldn't be bringing my home with me.

They just didn't know it yet.

Sitting on the couch as I accepted the offer to play profes-

185

sional football for the Chicago Bears, I held Grace's hand. Finn sat on my lap. My parents stood off to the side, wobbly grins on their faces. Ricky was there, and so were Landon and Emma. They surprised me by flying in for the day. Jon was across the room, sitting way too fucking close to Daisy. We'd need to talk about that real soon. Amy sat with the rest of my siblings, eating snacks and enjoying the excitement.

Even Marty and Corrine, Grace's parents, came. The road to forgiveness was still bumpy for my girl, but her parents were trying. Anyone who knew Finn loved him, and he could smooth over any rough patches. Unfortunately for them, Josh's parents didn't feel the same. Grace and her parents reached out to them, asking if they would like to meet Finn, but they refused. I thought Grace would be hurt, but my girl squared her shoulders and moved on. She had tried, for Josh and for Finn, and that was all she could do. The rest of us would make sure that those two had enough love to fill a football stadium.

The Bear's football stadium— Soldier Field.

And then some.

As soon as I hung up, screaming ensued. We hugged and slapped backs. I kissed my girl. And then we waited to hear it live and for it to be official.

All my life I thought this was the moment that would define me.

Until her. Until him. Until now.

They were my home. They were what defined me.

"Congratulations, baby," Grace whispered in my ear. "I'm so proud of you."

Andrew handed me a Bears cap and tossed one to Finn as well. "Bears?" Finn asked, taking in the hysteria around him. "Bears are my favorite animal ever!"

Grace and I laughed. Finn was the levity that I would always need in my life.

"Hey, pipe down!" I called out to the room. Everyone got

quiet, and I moved to the center. "Thank you all for being here. This room is filled with all my favorite people. But two people are the most special." I held out my hands and Grace took one, Finn grabbing onto the other. "They are my newest favorites." I reached down and picked Finn up, holding him against my hip. "And I know I want them by my side for the rest of my life." Grace covered her mouth with her hand, and I felt like the entire room held its collective breath.

Releasing my hold on Finn, I knelt on one knee and pulled the black velvet box from my pocket. Snapping it open, I held out the diamond solitaire I had chosen for my girl. "Grace Yeates, will you do me the honor of becoming my wife? Will you stay the strong, independent, mother and woman you are, but will you allow me to stand next to you? I want to be your partner, your best friend, and your love. Will you marry me?"

Grace fell to her knees and held my face with both of her hands. "Yes. I'm honored to marry you, Dean."

I removed her left hand from my cheek, kissed her fingers, and then slid on her ring. She mouthed "wow," and I chuckled. She had no idea what was in store for her in the future. I had a fat signing bonus to spoil her and Finn with now. First thing I was doing was buying her the most expensive bed she'd ever seen. Grace would never sleep on a couch again. Instead of saying any of this, I kissed her. Unfortunately it was a chaste kiss because Finn was right next to me. Everyone clapped and cheered some more, but I held up a finger. "Just Finn? Do I have your permission to marry your mama?"

Still kneeling, Grace and I were eye level with the little dude. His chin trembled, and he looked at us.

"Will you be my daddy now or just my Dean that loves me?" He sucked his lower lip into his mouth, and my own eyes got watery. Landon was going to ride me about my tears for the rest of my damn life.

"Since the first day I saw you on campus, running around as

super-Finn, I've thought you were special." I heard sniffling around me. "I would be honored to be your daddy on earth since you already have a daddy in heaven." I looked at Grace, and she didn't attempt to wipe away her tears. They ran down her face in streams even as she smiled as big and bright as I'd ever seen.

Finn kissed the "angel kiss" on his hand and grinned. "I have two daddies! And," he looked around the room, "four grandparents! And three aunts! And two uncles!" Finn pulled Grace's and my heads close to his. "I asked Santa for a big family," he whispered, but the room was so quiet I knew they could hear him. "It took him awhile to find you all, but that guy did it. Santa is the best."

Emma had been busy filling up glasses of champagne. We passed them around, and my dad held his high. "Dean, I know I'm not up on all the cool lingo you kids use, but I'd say this is hashtag winning."

My siblings shouted out boos and laughter. I groaned. "Dad, no. Just... no."

He grinned, no doubt thrilled that he could still embarrass me. "Alrighty then, to Santa!"

Laughter filled the room again as the sound of "cheers" and "to Santa" officially made this my favorite night of all time.

Epilogue

Grace

LANDON CAUGHT MY eye and motioned with a tilt of his head to the hallway leading into the kitchen. The celebration in the family room was rowdy, and the quiet of the empty room immediately relaxed me.

"Congratulations, darlin'. Let me see that rock."

I pressed my back against the wall to the kitchen and held my hand out in front of us. *Holy crap.* This ring was unreal. It was official. After I graduated next month, Finn and I were moving to Chicago.

Landon whistled. "Gorgeous. That tool beat me to it, proposing so soon. I have another year of school, so my Em's gotta wait until I graduate." He paused and then cleared his throat, looking right into my eyes. "I always knew a special girl would settle that wild man. I'm glad it was you. Just… take care of him, okay? The pros and the Bears… He has a lot of changes coming. He's gonna need you." Landon's eyebrows pulled together, and the smile fell from his face.

But my smile grew bigger. His best friend loved him too. "I'll watch out for him for the rest of my life, Landon. He's my blessing. I'll never forget that."

He grinned again. "I know that too. Girls like you and Em are different. In the best way." He laughed softly. "Hey, how are things going with your parents? I was surprised but happy for you to see them here."

Dean had filled me in on all the details about Landon's parents' estrangement from him after Christmas. I didn't think he'd reached out to them yet.

"They're..." I looked around the corner into the family room. Finn stood in front of my parents, animatedly telling them a story with his hands. Their faces reflected back pure joy. "Things are going well. They've apologized over and over again. We've talked over and over again. Things are still awkward. There's still pain in the words we said and the time we lost, but we're trying. They get to know Finn and Dean and... me. I realize now that they were missing out not knowing me. I'm worth knowing." I paused and looked into Landon's warm brown eyes. "You are too, Landon."

Silence filled the air between us, and then Landon wrapped his arms around me in a strong hug. "Dean's been a pain in my ass since we were six. Nothing better than knowing he has you though, Grace."

"Thanks, Landon. I'm so glad he has you too." We pulled apart, and Landon went into the family room, slipping his hand around Emma's.

I stood still, looking at my family, old and new, in the room. I had never known a love that could bring me to my knees, but also fill me with peace.

Until him.

Until Now.

Dear Reader,

Thank you for reading UNTIL NOW. If you enjoyed Dean and Grace's story, please leave a review! Reviews mean so much to an author.

Thank you,

Laura

Enjoy a preview of

Someday Soon

a novel by
LAURA WARD

Book **3** in the *Not Yet Series*
**This chapter is unedited and subject to change.

chapter
One

Daisy

"WHAT A SURPRISE. The fat cow's eating again." Belinda and Marley snickered behind me in line. I stiffened, squaring my shoulders, but kept my mouth shut. *Five more days.* I had five more days to go. I placed an apple next to my turkey sandwich and handed the cashier my card.

A hand shoved me forward and I whipped my head around. "Oops." Belinda's smirk was so mean, I shrank backwards a little.

"Move, you oaf. You think you're hot stuff, Daisy? You think your shit don't stink 'cause you got a hot-shot big brother playing football for the NFL?" Marley's face was pinched, her voice low. "Well you're not. You have always been and will always be a loser."

My eyes widened at the sight of my fifteen-year-old sister, Delilah, holding a large cup of soda over the back of Belinda's head. My older brother Damian moved next to her, with a matching cup of pop. In unison they poured the cups on top of Belinda and Marley. Both girls jumped away, clawing at their over-made-up faces as mascara and sticky soda streamed down their cheeks.

I slapped my hand across my face to hide my grin. My siblings loved to tease each other, but watch out if someone hurt one of us. Nothing bonded the Goldsmith clan like the need to protect our own.

"Let's go." Damian motioned with his chin and Delilah and I followed him out of the cafeteria and onto the outdoor patio. We sat at a picnic bench, the bright May sunlight warming our skin.

My brother and I were called Irish twins. My poor mother got pregnant with me when Damian was only a month old. Coupled with the fact that she was already saddled with a four-year-old terror named Dean and actual twins, two year old Devin and Dianna, I'm shocked she's still with us today.

Mom hung tough, in large part because all she and my Dad have ever wanted was to raise a family together. I was born nine months later and from the start, Damian and I had been tight. He looked out for me, his weird younger sister who never quite fit in. The Goldsmiths were loud, athletic, loud, and full of personality. Did I mention loud?

Regardless, Damian got me in a way the others didn't. But he was graduating in five days, too. He didn't need to spend his last days at Zionsville Academy watching out for me.

"Are you okay, Dais?" Delilah asked, her eyebrows furrowed with concern. "I heard a rumor that they were going to," she used her fingers to make air quotes, "take you down at lunch. I texted Damian and we took care of the bitches."

My stomach tightened. This was bullshit. I was her older sister and she shouldn't have to take care of me. I could handle my own problems. I'd been dealing with mean girls since middle school. But these days, I was just over it. I didn't have it left in me to care.

I shrugged. "I'm fine. You both shouldn't have done that. You're gonna get in trouble. It's not even your lunch shift, Delilah."

Damian picked up my apple and took a large bite. He chewed and then swallowed before speaking. "This is all the thanks I need." He waved at a group of girls that giggled as they walked by our table.

Damian was eighteen and pretty much a carbon copy of our oldest brother, Dean. Both played football their whole lives and both had scholarships to Indiana University to continue playing ball for the Hoosiers. They were both tall, fit, blond, and had egos the size of Mount Rushmore. But they also were the most protective guys I knew, other than my dad. I loved them like crazy. I adored all my family.

Which was why none of them understood why I needed to move away. But I did. I had to leave Indiana for a while. Find myself, perhaps? Years of dealing with girls like Belinda and Marley had me doubting myself and that pissed me off. I knew a few things with confidence and one of them was that I was smart. I finished all my required courses in three years and spoke to my parents about graduating high school early.

They protested at first. What about the dances I'd miss? The parties? Fact was, I was the lone Goldsmith who didn't do those things. High school social activity revolved around drinking and hooking up. Acting stupid and reckless. None of those things were me. I liked to read and I loved to cook.

Over the years, I'd lost friends who didn't understand that. Belinda and Marley were two of them. We'd been best friends when we were younger, but we'd changed. They wanted to hang out at my house, sneaking my college-aged sibling's beers and hooking up with my brothers. I had no interest in helping them achieve any of that. So while I spent my Saturdays perfecting my key lime pie recipe, they decided I was too weird to even be kind to.

In the end, my parents and I had compromised. I would get to graduate a year early, alongside Damian. I wanted to go to culinary school, preferably in an exotic, foreign location, but they wanted me to take a year off and work here in Indianapolis. I gave in when I realized that delaying my travels for one year was infinitely better than staying in high school.

"Crap, there's Principal Mahoney! I've gotta sneak back into Trigonometry class." Delilah ducked under the table and crawled to the side door. She slipped in before our Principal caught sight of her.

Damian laughed at her, but when he turned back to me, his face was sober. "Daisy, why do you let them treat you like that? The shit that comes out of their mouths is so rude. You know they're just jealous, right?"

My heart warmed. "They're not jealous, but thank you for saying that. I'm perfectly comfortable being different, Damian. But I'm also ready to move on. I'm over this town and this school." I stood up and gathered my uneaten lunch.

Damian tossed his apple core on to the tray. "Okay. Stay tough, sis. See you at home."

As I walked to the trash to dump the tray, my phone vibrated in my pocket. I pulled it out, resting my back against the brick wall of the school. As soon as I saw Jon's name, my heart raced in my chest.

I'd had a crush on Jon Roberts for as long as I could remember. Every fantasy of every love story that I had ever conjured up in my mind involved him. He was a bit shorter than the guys in my family, but at six feet, he still had a couple of inches on me. He was stockier, thicker than any guy I knew. Jon was bulky with muscle. His biceps were so big, I was sure he intimidated everyone else at the gym. I pictured those arms lifting me up into his embrace and closed my eyes.

There was a reason Belinda and Marley called me names referring to my weight. I looked different than any other girl my age in high school. I wasn't fat, I knew that. But I was … curvy. Everywhere. My breasts were large, a full D cup. My hips were round and my ass stuck out. Some guys loved it, yelling comments when I was at the mall or out walking down the street.

I hated it. Why couldn't I look like Dianna or Delilah or my Mom? They were skinny bean poles, petite with tiny breasts and no butt to mention. They fit in. No parts stuck out like a flashing neon sign. None of them had to hear cat calls or the lewd comments posted on Instagram or Snapchat when I dared to post a picture.

Part of what fueled my fantasy about Jon was that he was the only guy I knew who looked like he could handle me. His hands were large, and when I pictured him holding me close… I fit. With him.

But those were only fantasies. Jon was Dean's best friend. He was also twenty-three. Being that I was still seventeen for another two months, my fantasy had no chance of ever happening. There was also the small fact that he had no clue how I felt about him. Or if he did, he ignored it. He clearly felt nothing but friendship towards me.

Opening my eyes, I looked down at the phone.

Jon: *Hey. How's your day going?*
Me: *Not great. I'm so done with school.*
Jon: *Girls bugging you?*

I had made the colossal mistake of confiding in Jon late last summer about how bad my so-called-friends had gotten. The texts, phone calls, and messages on social media were reaching a frustrating peak. He'd talked with me for hours one night while Dean hooked up with Stephanie in our basement.

We had sat outside, looking at the stars and I had unloaded on him. Jon sipped his beer and listened to me. Really listened. He was the only non-family member who had ever done that for me.

He told me that I was special. Pretty. And that he could say that or my parents could say that, but none of that would matter until I believed it about myself. He told me to steel my heart and my head from their comments and focus on the real me. On what I loved to do and who I wanted to be.

I remembered every second of that conversation because that was when I realized I loved Jon.

And that he would never, could never feel the same.

Me: *They were. D & D poured soda on their heads. Cooled them off. Ha!*

Jon: *Nice. Plans later?*

Me: *Nope. Cooking dinner for the fam. Chicken cacciatore, homemade noodles, asparagus with hollandaise sauce. You want some?*

Jon: *You had me at the noodles. See you later.*

A little game I played with myself was to guess what food would make Jon come over for dinner. It wasn't too hard. Since his graduation from IU last month, he'd moved back home. Even though Dean was living in Chicago, getting ready to train with the Bears, Jon still joined us for dinner many nights a week. My parents loved him.

We all did.

My love for him just didn't feel familial or platonic anymore.

Interestingly, Jon would be in the same predicament as me next year. His plan was to attend law school, but first he needed to save up for a year, working as a law clerk at a downtown law firm before taking his exams and applying to schools.

An hour later, the final bell rang and I headed out the front doors of the building. Damian and Delilah had texted me that Principal Mahoney was sending them to detention for the soda pop debacle. No one was surprised, but my siblings would take a month of detention to protect me. I wished they didn't have to.

I turned right, walking toward town. When I needed to cook, I'd wander around the specialty grocery stores for a few hours, using my babysitting money to buy vinegars and herbs that excited no one in the house but me. I'd call my Mom when I was ready, and she or my Dad would pick me up, helping me cart my edible treasures home.

I crossed the street, leaving my school day behind me. I walked for a few minutes before entering the parking lot of our local grocery store. A low whistle off to my side startled me. I froze, bracing myself for the comments or jeers.

"Need help picking out the best asparagus?"

Leaning against the door to his truck, keys twirling around his finger, was the most delicious sight I'd ever laid eyes on.

Jon.

I swallowed, my mouth and throat dry. "Jon?" My voice was squeaky.

The corner of Jon's mouth lifted in a grin. He wore black sunglasses, so I couldn't tell if he rolled his eyes at my nervousness or found it funny. He straightened, walking to me slowly.

"What are you doing here?" My fingers tangled in front of me. God, Daisy. Calm down.

He stood so close that his scent surrounded me. He smelled faintly of a masculine cologne, mixed with soap, and the leather of a football. Leaning forward his lips brushed my cheek and I stopped breathing.

Oh God. Kiss me. Kiss me. Kiss me.

He didn't kiss me.

"Thought you might like some company. Rough days suck." Jon wrapped an arm around my shoulder and hugged me to his side as we walked toward the store.

I nodded, blinking back my hot tears. Why was I crying? Belinda and Marley no longer made me sad. But Jon caring about me? Thinking about me? That caused a torrent of emotions to bubble to the surface.

Jon stopped walking. He faced me, lifting his sunglasses on top of his head. His warm brown eyes sparkled in the late day sun. "You're better than them, Daisy. Never forget that. You're perfect just like you are. Five more days, sunshine. You can make it five more days."

Sunshine? A nickname? Swoon.

I wiped my tears away furiously. "Of course. Five more days."

Jon wrapped his arms around me in a tight hug. I hesitated for a second. Should I hug him back? Could I hold him close and not let my body push for more? Whatever. I stopped second-guessing myself and hugged him back. I pulled myself into his embrace, burying my face in his neck and breathing him in.

I could get through five more *years* of high school with a daily dose of this.

Jon's body became rigid and he moved back quickly. I stumbled with him and he held my forearm to keep me balanced.

"Sorry." He slipped his glasses back on his face looking to his left and right. "Should we start shopping?"

My stomach dropped. Too much, Daisy. Too damn much.

"'Course. Let's go pick some asparagus, shall we?"

I turned my attention toward my favorite hobby and forced myself to stop focusing on my favorite guy.

Good luck asparagus. You've got your work cut out for you tonight.

acknowledgements

The first person to thank is my sweet husband who encourages me to fulfill my dreams! Thank you and I love you!

Thank you to my children for understanding when I need to work or travel. Most importantly, thank you for sharing my love of books and writing. You three are the best and I love you more each day.

To my wonderful beta readers: Amanda Rounsaville, Bekky Levesque, Dani Fisher, Pat Rosner, Stacey Lynn, Tamara Debbaut, and Christine Manzari–thank you for allowing me to pick your brains, ask you endless questions and for providing the most helpful feedback.

I would like to give a special shout out to my cousins Matt Krebs and Meagan Lee. Matt talked me through all the football, agents, drafts, and sports technicalities in the book. Meagan read through an early draft to make sure my Bloomington/IU references were spot on. Thank you both so much!

After the first drafts of a book are finished, the real work begins. Luckily I have the best team to help me. Working with Amy Donnelly at Alchemy and Words was invigorating! You are an incredible editor. Thank you for your time and care with my story. Thanks to Victory Editing for proofreading. Your attention to detail is awesome. Regina Wamba at Mae I Design found this beautiful image and created the cover. Thank you! The exceptional formatting in the ebook and paperback versions of this book are because of Julie Titus at JT Formatting. She is amazing! Tamara Debbaut is the creative genius behind my marketing artwork and I appreciate her help so much. Finally, I would like to thank Southern Belle Book Productions for planning my cover reveal and book tour.

While I'm at it, there are a few bloggers who have been instrumental in sharing my books. Thanks to Candy from Prisoners of Print, Erin from Southern Belle, Denise from Shh Mom's Reading, Gitte and Jenny from TotallyBookedBlog, Jamie and Theresa from Smokin'Hot Reads, Tash from Book Lit Love, Jennifer from Just Me & My Kindle, Jenn from Garden of REden, Stephenee from Nerd Girl Reviews, Alicia from Mean Girls Love Books, and Ethan from One Guy's Guide to Good Reads.

Tamara Debbaut there aren't enough way to say thank you to you! You are there for me with any questions, problems, issues, or ideas I have. Thank you for your talent and friendship!

Christine, what can I say? Meeting you, writing with you, and traveling with you has been the greatest blessing I've received from this journey. You are the most generous and talented lady I know. Thank you for ALWAYS being there for me.

Finally, to anyone reading this right now–you have made my dreams come true. I'm a writer thanks to you!